FIRST DATES AND BIRTHDAY CAKES

ISABEL MURRAY

Copyright © 2024 by Isabel Murray

All rights reserved.

No part of this book may be reproduced in any form or by any electronic or mechanical means, including information storage and retrieval systems, without written permission from the author, except for the use of brief quotations in a book review.

This is a work of fiction. Names, characters, places, and incidents either are the product of the author's imagination or are used fictitiously. Any resemblance to actual persons, living or dead, events, or locales is entirely coincidental.

Cover content is used for illustrative purposes only and any person depicted on the cover is a model.

First paperback edition June 2024

FIRST DATES AND BIRTHDAY CAKES

Ben Porter is turning forty, and he's not being cool about it.

He told his friends and family that he wanted to let this particular milestone pass by without any fuss, and for once, they actually listened.

Which is great. Because now here he is, sitting in his kitchen on a rainy Saturday morning, all alone, and he can *feel* himself aging.

So he decides to do something about it.

And maybe throwing himself a last-minute ice-skating party for one in an attempt to recreate the carefree birthdays of his expired youth wasn't the best idea. Or the most normal. He'd even go so far as to say it was a terrible idea, as there's a non-zero chance that his impromptu birthday activity will turn into an impromptu birthday trip to the hospital. Because despite the fact that he remembers being pretty hot stuff at skating?

He's not. He's really, *really* not.

He's so incredibly bad at it that a tall, gorgeous member of staff—who actually *is* pretty hot stuff—has to come over and scrape him off the ice, just so he stops ruining everyone else's Saturday.

Except Jake isn't a member of staff, he has an ulterior (romantic!) motive for helping Ben, and Ben's worst birthday ever is about to take a surprising turn for the better...

∼

First Dates and Birthday Cakes is a 33k-word romantic comedy novella with a midlife crisis, a big surprise that Ben really should have seen coming, and something that looks a whole lot like happily ever after.

1

Somewhere outside my bedroom window, a thrush greeted the dawn with a truly obnoxious degree of enthusiasm.

I sighed and flopped onto my back, taking my phone with me. Holding it up in front of my face, I stared at it, unblinking.

My regular Saturday alarm would go off in a couple of hours at eight a.m., as it did every Saturday.

This wasn't a normal Saturday.

This was a very specific Saturday, and to mark the very special occasion about to occur, I'd woken early and set a timer. A countdown, if you will.

Here we go.

Ten seconds left. Nine. Eight...

I watched the screen as the numbers flicked down to zero. The alarm blared.

Well.

That was it. It was over. Over and done with.

I just turned forty.

R.I.P. to my youth.

I slapped the alarm off, hauled the duvet up around my ears, and hunkered in.

∽

THE PHONE ON MY BEDSIDE TABLE RANG. I IGNORED IT.

After it had stopped and started three more times, I got the hint. Ravi wasn't going to give up.

I stuck my hand out, dragged my phone back under the covers with me, and accepted the call.

"*Happy birthday to youuuuuuu—*" he began.

"Ravi, you know I hate that song."

"*Happy birthday to youuuuuu!*"

"Stop singing."

"*Happy birthday, dear Benjamiiiiiin!*"

"I'm hanging up."

"No, you're not. *Happy birthday to you!* I love you."

I scowled into the darkness and mumbled, "I love you, too."

"Aw. Thanks, buddy. All right. How are you doing today?"

"How am I doing? I just summited life, that's how I'm doing. I'm standing at the top of a mountain and it's all downhill from here. Obviously, I'm doing *great*."

"Ben, are you freaking out?"

"Pfft," I said. "No."

"It sounds like you might be."

And it sounded like he was smiling about it.

I glared at my phone. "I'm not freaking out. Why would I freak out? It's not as if my life is over. It's not as if my youth is a memory. It's not as if I somehow turned into a forty-year-old civil engineer with high blood pressure, enough grey hairs that I can't even pretend they're not there anymore,

First Dates and Birthday Cakes | 3

and a mortgage I'll be paying off until I'm sixty. If I even make it to sixty."

While I was on a roll and complaining about things, I had also absolutely failed to acquire the loving partner with whom I was supposed to walk into the sunset of my life, hand in aged hand.

From what the internet had to say about what I could expect as a (newly) middle-aged man, that was pretty much it. If I hadn't found it by now, I'd missed my chance. I should go ahead and resign myself to a life of unending solitude.

"That's the kind of positive, can-do attitude I like to hear," Ravi said.

"It's my birthday. I don't have to be positive today. I don't have to do anything. I can live my truth, Ravi. I can lie here in bed all day and be quietly and understandably devastated at the loss of my youth if I want to."

"You're not living your truth. You're having a midlife crisis."

"I am not having a midlife crisis. How *dare* you."

I was definitely having a midlife crisis.

"Mm-hmm."

"I'm merely standing back, having a good look at my life. Taking stock." And I was coming up empty.

"Well, you can cut that shit out right now. Don't stand still and look back. Get up and move forwards! The best is yet to come!"

"You don't know that."

"I do know that. This year, Ben? Trust me. This year is going to be the very best year of your life."

Ravi and his parents had moved in next door when I was three years old, and it was hate at first sight.

My mother, thrilled to discover that the new neighbour had a son only a few months younger than me, had invited

Ravi's mum over for coffee and cake. The unsuspecting women settled themselves on the patio to watch a baby bromance unfold, and instead, toddler war broke out.

Ravi started it.

He was big into monster trucks at that age, probably because he had the personality of one, and the first thing he did was select his favourite, trot over to where I was busy ignoring him and playing with my own toys, and clobber me with it.

As a budding engineer, I was more into construction myself, and I retaliated by upending my bumper-sized bucket of Duplo bricks on his head.

Bricks and trucks were tossed about, teddy bears got involved, hair was pulled, someone got so upset they had a toilet emergency in their Pull-Ups (I say Ravi, he says me) and by the time we were separated, our horrified mothers had made a pact to keep us apart.

They were shit at keeping pacts, because a month later Ravi was invited to my fourth birthday party, we bonded over jelly and ice cream, and the rest was history.

Every birthday since then, without fail, he'd been telling me that this year was going to be the most amazing year yet.

I'd stopped believing him a while ago, but I did appreciate his unflagging enthusiasm.

"God, I wish you were gay," I sighed. "Why couldn't you have been gay? We'd have had such a beautiful life together." Also, Ravi was a trauma surgeon. With the kind of money he pulled in per year, we'd have already paid off the mortgage.

He snorted. "Even if I was gay, you'd kill me in my damn sleep if we got together," he said. "I'm very demanding in bed."

I very much enjoyed men demanding things of me in

bed. I wasn't about to tell Ravi that and give him any more ammunition to tease me with. He already had more than enough.

"You're my soulmate," I told him glumly.

"You're really feeling it today, huh?"

"Yes."

"You're my soulmate, too. And this year you'll find another soulmate. One who doesn't mind giving you a good dicking."

"You are *so* crass sometimes," I said. "I was being meaningful, and you made it about dicks."

Under his boisterous laughter, I heard a soft murmur.

"Ravi," I said through gritted teeth, "please tell me you're not pep-talking me through my very personal midlife crisis with one of your girlfriends lying there listening."

"Oh, *now* it's a midlife crisis?" he said. There was another murmur. "Right. Ben, Lizzie would like you to know that she's not stupid enough to be my girlfriend, she's just using me for sex because she's out of batteries and couldn't be arsed to go to the twenty-four hour garage for more last night, and she'll see you—hah. Soon. She'll see you soon."

Not if I saw her first.

Lizzie was an occupational therapist who often worked with Ravi's patients once he'd finished putting them back together. She was the type of organised, practical woman who did an hour of yoga every weekday morning to greet the dawn, and ran marathons at the weekends to relax. I wasn't ashamed to admit that she intimidated the shit out of me.

"Okay," Ravi said, "some of us have to work today, so we'd better wrap it up. The people of Oxfordshire and the surrounding counties are out and about, injuring themselves as we speak, and I will no doubt be in surgery most of the day. Are you gonna make it without me?"

"Uh, yes, I think I can manage," I said, and congratulated myself on how genuinely unaffected I sounded.

Inside, I died a little.

For the first time ever, I wouldn't get to see him on my actual birthday.

And I knew it was weird for someone of my advanced age to get hung up on, but seriously. For thirty-seven years straight, there he had been, by my side. My emotional support extrovert, my BFF, my ride or die.

All good things came to an end, I supposed.

"See you tomorrow?" I said. We'd planned to meet up in Oxford for a swanky dinner at The Randolph—Ravi's treat, because I couldn't afford it. Even if I could, I had better things to do with my money than swallow it.

"See you then. Have a great day!"

"Not likely," I muttered as he hung up, no doubt to fall on Lizzie like the insatiable animal he was before they both had to get out of bed and save lives and whatnot.

While I hung out at home.

Alone.

Ravi was working over the weekend. My parents had stayed at home in Scotland, and I'd scheduled a trip up to see them next month. I'd made it very clear to Molly the office manager when she cornered me last week that I preferred not to undergo the whole awkward cake-and-cards business, and got one card signed by everyone and a couple of hugs at the end of work yesterday.

Well, I deserved what I got. I'd insisted that I didn't want a fuss made, and for once, everyone had actually listened.

I clambered out of bed and shuffled into the bathroom, testing my hips to see if they were creaking yet. No creaks. I did a squat, and scowled when my knees cracked on the way up.

Didn't mean anything. They always did that.

I got into the shower and turned it to as cold as I could stand because I'd heard good things about the anti-ageing benefits.

I lasted about thirty wretched seconds before I turned the dial back up to my usual hot and steamy.

Once upon a time, I'd loved birthdays.

I'd loved the sheer, uncomplicated fun of them—the parties and the presents. More than that, I'd loved the magic of them—the excitement, the possibility, the promise of good times ahead.

I didn't know when or how it had all faded away.

Although fifteen years of being a civil engineer and twenty years of paying taxes probably had something to do with it.

Being an adult was hard. The older you got, the harder it got.

It was simpler when I was a child.

If this was, say, my tenth birthday, then today would feel very different.

Instead of standing grumpily in the tub under the shower spray with my head bowed like Eeyore, I'd be rushing about getting all excited about my party, about spending time with friends and opening presents.

If I remembered correctly, my tenth birthday was the one when we rented out the ice rink.

I smiled at the memory.

I'd been pretty darned good at ice skating. Ravi had barely been able to stop clinging to the sides, but I'd whooshed around, revelling in the cold air, the disco music, the happy shouts and screams.

And it wasn't as if I wanted to turn the clock back and be a child again. I liked my independence far too much.

There were lots of good things about being an adult. While I couldn't think of a single example right now, I knew there were.

It stood to reason that there were also lots of good things about being a forty-plus adult. There was at least a chance that Ravi was right. This could indeed be the very best year of my life.

It was hard to believe, I thought as I sat at my kitchen table drinking my third cup of coffee and beginning to vibrate from the caffeine overload, when every other birthday card I opened—and there weren't even that many, as most people these days texted—was an ageist joke.

I was seriously side-eyeing the greetings card industry at this point. Someone ought to do something.

Once I'd propped all the cards up on the table and tossed the envelopes in the recycling bin, I swiped through the notifications on my phone, responding to early birthday texts with emojis of thumbs-ups and clinking glasses of champagne.

And then my mother called.

I stared at the screen.

For a craven moment, I considered not answering. A moment only; she was worse than Ravi. She'd keep calling me if I didn't pick up. She'd get in the car and drive over to check on me, and I didn't want that. It was three-hundred-plus miles down a busy motorway from my parents' house in Scotland to my house in Chipping Fairford.

"Darling!" Mum screeched.

I winced when a sharp *pop-pop-pop* noise went off. "Morning, Mum."

First Dates and Birthday Cakes | 9

"That was your father pulling a party popper, by the way," she said. "Right in my ear."

I could tell. She was yelling unnecessarily loudly. I turned the volume of my phone down.

"Happy birthday!"

"Thank you."

There was an expectant silence.

"And thank you for my existence," I said dutifully.

I'd said it once as a snotty, sarcastic teen, and she'd made me do it every year since.

"I'm so sorry for compromising your pelvic floor. I appreciate the stretch marks, saggy boobs and hollowed-out bones you bear in my service. Etc., etc."

"You're half-arsing it, Ben, but never mind. You're welcome. Now. Are you in bed still?"

"Nope."

"Good," she said, sounding enthusiastic and encouraging. It was the same voice she used on all the rescue dogs Dad fostered since he'd retired from being a vet. "*Good* boy."

"Mum."

She sighed. "Ben, I don't want you to be dramatic about your birthday."

"I'm not being dramatic. I'm sitting at my kitchen table, drinking coffee, looking at my phone. Very calmly."

"I was worried I'd have to come over there and drag you out from under your duvet."

"No need," I said. "I am resigned. It's just another day, after all. No biggie. Nothing special happening today. Just one more circuit of this wretched rock circling the sun."

"Oh, good," she said dryly. "That lovely cliche. What's next? *I don't see what's so great about me not dying for another three hundred and sixty-five days?*"

"You know," I said at her very poor imitation of me,

"some people's mother's call their offspring, sing happy birthday to them, and hang up. They don't start by trying to give them a heart attack with party poppers, then get mean and sarcastic."

"Those poor children," she said.

I grinned at the phone. "I love you, Mum."

"I love you too, sweetheart." There was a brief pause and the sound of someone speaking in the background. "And your father sends his regards," she added.

Dad was more reticent about expressing his affection but I was confident I could swap out *regards* for *love* here. "Thanks, Dad," I said loudly.

Mum giggled like a girl, then squealed. "No! Barry! This is my phone call, make your own."

I heard some more giggling as they presumably tussled for the phone before Dad gave up and shouted, "Happy birthday, Benji! We'll see you—"

Mum screeched again—I did *not* want to know what caused that painful and sudden increase in volume, thanks —and said, "Soon! We'll see you soon, darling. Have a wonderful day. Don't do anything too wild and crazy!"

I hung up and sat there, listening to the second hand of my kitchen clock tick loudly on in my empty kitchen. Light rain pattered on the window. The bedraggled squirrel in my walnut tree chattered with fury as it kept reaching for and failing to grab a nut.

That bloody thrush was still singing its little heart out.

Wild and crazy?

That'd be nice.

I'd had more than a few wild and crazy birthdays over the years. More than my fair share, even. Ravi had seen to that. I'd been hot-air ballooning over Bavaria, went on an ill-advised pub-crawl in Budapest, bungee jumped in Spain.

That had been back in our twenties, though. It was hard to schedule fun around our busy careers—especially Ravi's, the over-achiever.

This year, I realised, it really was all over. It was the end of an era. This birthday would set the tone for the rest of my life.

It was going to be...sedate.

Instead of flying off somewhere exotic to get bullied into flinging myself off a cliff, or climbing into a basket under a giant balloon to drink champagne two thousand feet above the ground, or even staying local and getting another tattoo on my arse that I'd have to get lasered off a month later, like the regrettable *Jurassic Park* T-Rex one I got when I was twenty-nine, I had a quiet day ahead.

A quiet, lonely day, most likely followed by an early night with my Kindle, and then the very adult and age-appropriate celebration at a sophisticated restaurant in a posh hotel that Ravi had planned.

I shifted in my chair.

God, it sounded sad.

The second hand ticked on.

Of course, I could always do something wild and crazy on my own. If I wanted to. I didn't need Ravi to come up with it or organise it.

Besides, dinner at The Randolph? What was that about? He'd taken his *mum* to dinner for her seventieth.

I didn't have to sit here and not do anything for my birthday, other than speak to my parents and my best friend on the phone, just because I was regretting the fact that I'd downplayed it too hard and people really were leaving me to mope.

I didn't have to accept it being sedate.

I could be cool and independent.

I was inventive and imaginative, too. I could be punk about this.

Not too punk, though.

There were limits.

It was far too late in the day to book a flight anywhere and I had to be in the office at nine o'clock on Monday morning. Whisking myself off for an impromptu city break was off the table.

Also, it was Saturday, and everyone I knew was already busy doing their Saturday things. Throwing myself a birthday party, even a small get-together, was out.

I was more of a party attendee than a party thrower, anyway.

I stared out of the rain-streaked window. The squirrel in the walnut tree gave up on stretching for the nut and sat back on its haunches to scream at it in primal rage instead.

I could...?

If not a party, I could do a birthday activity? Hmm. Something solo.

And that thought right there, I would come to realise, was the point upon which my destiny turned.

Because I could have chosen any number of things to do. Things that were meaningful, or self-indulgent or, at the very least, normal.

I could have gone to a spa and paid people to pamper me all day long. I could have caught the train into London and headed to the British Museum to gaze upon the marvels of the Ancient World, and had a revelation about Man and His Complicated Place in the grand scheme of things.

I could have got another dinosaur tattoo on my arse.

I didn't do anything like that.

I flipped through my mental Rolodex (oh *god*, I was so old, I knew what a Rolodex was. Never had one, but knew what one was) and reviewed past birthdays, seeking inspiration.

I didn't have to flip far.

One memory leaped out at me—perhaps because I'd already revisited it in the shower earlier—and the moment I thought it, my heart seized upon it and said: *yes*.

That is exactly *what a totally normal person would choose to do on their fortieth birthday.*

It's cool. It's edgy. It will rekindle your youthful joie de vivre.

So I got into my car and drove to the ice rink where I'd held my tenth birthday party.

I discovered that in direct contrast to what my memories said, I couldn't actually skate for shit, I made an idiot out of myself, and I earned a butt-full of bruises with matching ones for kneecaps and elbows.

Oh, and while I was doing all that, I also met the love of my life.

Best stupid idea ever.

2

The ice rink in Milton Keynes was further from Chipping Fairford than the rink in Oxford, but it was significantly bigger. It was still—perhaps predictably—packed on a Saturday afternoon, and as for the parking? A total nightmare.

Even so, my enthusiasm remained undimmed as I handed over my shoes in exchange for a pair of bright blue plastic rental skates, and waddled my ungainly way to the edge of the rink. I hesitated as I surveyed the bustling crowd of families, friend groups and couples thronging the ice, but even the way I felt quite suddenly and conspicuously alone didn't put me off.

I continued to be convinced that this was a fabulous idea, right up to the moment I stepped confidently through the gate onto the rink, my blades kissed the ice, and I went from vertical to horizontal so quickly, it shocked the breath clean out of me.

I groaned quietly and lay there, trying to get my bearings.

At least I'd fallen away from the gate and wasn't causing

an obstruction or spoiling anyone else's fun. I could tell by the way the two kids and tired-looking father who'd been stuffed up behind me as I made my bold debut onto the ice swished right on past without stopping.

It was fine. I didn't need help.

I could definitely get up on my own.

I slither-shuffled on hands and knees further from the gate and pushed up to a kneeling position.

The blood in my cheeks throbbed in time to the banging pop music blaring from the sound system. I looked around and was relieved to see that no one was paying me any attention whatsoever.

At the other side of the rink across from me, a girl with long brown hair squealed happily as she fell. Her friend laughed and pulled her up.

No one gave her a second look.

A teen trying to impress the boy next to him as they passed me attempted to spin around mid-stride and go backwards. He did a quick, skittering running-man instead, before he wiped out and the boy tripped over him.

No one looked at them, either.

All right. Falling was acceptable. It was normal.

Getting up, however? How was I even supposed to do this?

Thank god I was at the edge of the rink and had the barrier to push against. If I'd fallen out there on the open ice without a friend to help me up, I'd have no chance. I'd have to army-crawl my way to the side, or more likely I'd be stuck flopping around until the Zamboni came and cleared the ice, scooting me ahead of it.

I reached for the top of the barrier and heaved myself to my feet.

Feet which immediately tried to go in opposite directions.

I clung on, I skidded around, I used every muscle in my core and some in my inner thighs I hadn't known I possessed until now, and I made it.

Upright!

Pretending that I hadn't already been lapped by the tired dad and his two kids, I took a moment.

Okay.

I was here.

I was having fun.

Fun was being had.

My confidence was rattled, but it was fine. It was like riding a bike. Once you learn, you never forget.

I inched my away along, clutching the barrier and dragging myself hand over hand.

Any minute now, my skills would kick back in and I'd join the happy, laughing crowd. Any minute now, I, too, would be zipping around with a big smile on my face, cheeks red from cold and exertion rather than embarrassment.

Maybe I'd get into skating in a big way. Take lessons. Get amazing.

And while I couldn't see me *doing* anything with my skills once I'd got amazing, I'd heard that skating did fabulous things for your arse. It couldn't hurt to tighten things up back there. I'd been slacking on the squats and lunges during my workouts recently, and it was starting to show.

A favourite tune came on over the speakers. I bopped my head cautiously.

Who needed the gym? Who needed a treadmill, or an elliptical? Why sit on an unpleasantly damp padded bench and heave weights up and down when instead, I could move my body to the music and glide around like a graceful, prowling ice panther.

Like *that* guy.

I spared the man a quick glance as he buzzed past for the third time. Our eyes met, his lips curled, and then he was gone.

He was tall. Muscular but lean, not bulky. Definitely prowling and graceful. Make that insultingly graceful. Way too at his ease when some of us ice panthers were still hauling themselves laboriously around while their bodies were remembering how to do it. His attitude was very in your face. He even had his hands in his pockets, the dick.

I wobbled and clutched at the barrier.

Concentrate.

You know what? This *was* fun. I was enjoying myself. I'd found my feet and I was steady now. More or less. The air, chilled from the ice, felt nice against my skin. I began to smile. I wasn't half bad at this, and I—

I ran out of barrier.

I stopped smiling and my eyes widened.

The bottom end of the rink had been cordoned off with cones to create an enclosed space for the toddlers and small kids. A whole gaggle of them were out there, shoving their skating aids about, their fat little legs working furiously as they scuttled over the ice behind rigid plastic penguins and polar bears with handles coming out of their necks.

Some of the children were sitting down, chilling. Others stood around, looking baffled.

It was cute and adorable, but *wow*. Selfish. How was I supposed to get to the barrier on the other side?

I had to go out onto open ice.

Nope.

No.

Time to backtrack.

I turned around, immediately got shoulder-checked by a blond kid with acne and a murderous scowl, and hit the ice.

I blinked up at the metal beams in the ceiling overhead.

So.

This rink was on a one-way system. Made sense.

I hauled myself back up and took a moment to assess the lay of the land.

If I was very, very careful—and if everyone around me was also very, very careful, and didn't take me out—I could cross over to the other side of the rink.

If I fell? Big deal. I fell.

I wouldn't enjoy scrabbling on hands and knees along the line of plastic cones across what looked like a hundred feet of ice, being sneered at by teens, grinned at by kids, and having parents make a yikes face as they passed by, but I *could* do it.

I let go of the barrier one reluctant finger at a time. I checked behind me then fixed my gaze on the opposite side of the rink, flipped out a hand to indicate I was on the move, checked behind me once more, and pulled out into the stream of happy people.

And…I was doing it.

Wow.

I was doing it.

This was great. *Oh.* I felt great.

I was bold and brave and halfway across the ice.

This was a fabulous idea. It was a fantastic start to my forties. I was engaged, present, fully in my body and in the moment.

From here on in, I vowed, no more bemoaning my age, no more being glum about everything I'd failed to do or acquire. Nothing but clear, crisp positivity. I was embracing my next decade of life with open arms and a tender kiss on the lips, and—

"Whoops. Hah. Sorry, mate."

I hit the ice flat on my back and the radiant young couple who'd decked me skated on without a second look.

Fuck.

Fucking *fuck*.

Before I could even roll over and attempt to get up without the assistance of the barrier, someone whooshed to a stop right beside me, and said, "Are you okay?"

I wiped the small spray of snow from my face and glared up at the guy. It was the arrogant ice panther. Of course it was. "Sure."

I couldn't tell with any degree of accuracy from my position on my back, but he had to be over six feet tall. An ungodly amount of it seemed to be leg. He towered over me like a colossus.

Like a giant, blond, handsome colossus.

"Is this your phone?" He dropped into a squat as easily if he was in a yoga studio, not balanced on blades, and scooped it up.

It must have shot out of my back pocket when I landed on my arse. Ravi was always on at me not to put it there, especially after I'd dropped it down the toilet—twice

"Shit," I said, and groaned my way up to sitting. "Is it cracked?"

He checked it out. "Nope. Looks good." He turned it over and smiled at the *Jurassic Park* stickers on the back. "Dinosaur fan or film fan?"

Was he laughing at me?

"Both," I said.

He gave it back and I quickly stuffed it in my pocket.

Straightening, he held out a big hand. "Let's get you up, hey?"

"I'm fine," I said.

I was not fine and we both knew it. People zoomed by. Music played on. He looked at me. I looked at him.

"You need any help?" he asked, raising his brows.

"Nope." I flailed my legs around and got absolutely nowhere. "This is easier with something to hold onto," I told him. After a short crab walk and some more flailing while he stood over me and watched with interest, I slumped. "Maybe I could do with a little help," I said. "How am I even supposed to do this?"

"It's not that hard. Get on your hands and knees for me."

He returned my suspicious squint with an innocent look. "And then what?" I asked.

"I'll get you on your feet. Come on. Let's go."

I did as he suggested, and the moment I was on all fours, strong hands fitted around my waist and he plucked me up off the ice.

"*Ahhh*." My legs skittered like Bambi's but he held me tight, even when I bounced off his very firm chest and somehow got a leg between his thick thighs.

"Stop struggling," he said with amusement.

It was tough, but I managed. Then I realised that I'd plastered myself to his front, I was clutching his extremely hard biceps, and I had to tip my head back to meet his gaze.

His eyes were blue.

They'd looked dark from where I lay sprawled at his feet, but this close, I could see that they were an incredible navy blue.

"Okay?" he said, after I'd stared at him like the creepiest person on the planet without saying a word for what felt like a full minute but was probably only about ten agonisingly awkward seconds.

"Yes. Great. Thanks." I continued to clutch him.

He smiled again. This one was slower. Warmer. "Need some help getting over to the side?"

"I'd like to say that I can take it from here, but I think that would be overly optimistic of me."

"No problem," he said, and turned us in a quick, tight circle.

I shrieked.

I shrieked so loudly that the trio of tweens giggling their way past us all turned as one with appalled stares.

He was trying hard not to laugh.

"Warn a guy," I snapped.

"Sorry. Ready to go?"

He skated slowly backwards, drawing me after him.

My feet went out from under me, I lurched forwards, and I body-slammed him. "No."

I should just ask him to carry me. It wasn't like I had any dignity left.

He peeled me off him, set me back, and said with patience, "Let's go again."

I heaved a sigh. "You're not going to believe this, but I *can* skate."

"I don't believe it." He moved off again and I shuffled after him. He squeezed my arms above the elbows, where he was holding me firmly.

He had big hands. Big, warm, confident hands.

"Stop looking at your feet," he said.

I wasn't looking at my feet, I was looking at his hands. I quickly looked at my feet. "I'm trying not to trip you up."

"You let me worry about that. Don't look down."

"I hate that phrase. No one ever says it unless you're in peril."

He huffed a laugh. "You are not in peril."

"Tell that to my arse. It is going to be absolutely covered in bruises tomorrow. And my elbows." They'd made a heck of a noise, cracking down on the ice earlier.

He didn't say anything until I glanced up. "Yeah. That's it. Look at me. Keep looking at me."

I did. Mostly because I couldn't look away.

Something gently bumped against my back. He'd manoeuvred me across the ice and got me safely to the barrier without me even noticing, let alone falling. "Oh," I said. "Thank you."

He stared down at me.

This close, the height difference was much more noticeable.

I was a gangly five-eleven on a good day. In other words, not today. Today, my core was clenched with tension and my shoulders were rounded protectively. It made a difference. It took off an inch. Today, I was probably only hitting five-ten. He had to be nudging six-three.

I bet he went down like a redwood.

"It must really hurt when you fall over," I said.

He cocked his head.

I gestured from the ice all the way up the length of his body. "You're tall. Must be like a tree falling."

His lips were a lovely deep pink. The lower one was fuller and he had a pronounced Cupid's bow. They tipped up at the edges as he leaned in and said, like he was sharing a secret, "I don't fall over much. I'm very good at skating."

"Are you?" Was it me or did I sound breathless?

"Yes."

"Me too. I mean, I used to be."

He gave me that disbelieving look again as he glided back a foot and turned to lean against the barrier beside me, tipping his head down to keep his eyes on mine. He spread his arms wide and lounged, relaxed and comfortable.

"I did! It's been a few years. I thought it would all come back. It didn't."

"How long is a few years?"

"Uh. Thirty? Thirty years." I winced when I realised I'd just confessed to being decrepit.

"In that case, perhaps you need to be on the ice for more than ten minutes before you can say you gave your skills a chance to come back."

"Ten minutes?" I checked my watch. "My god. It felt like I was out there forever."

"You want to give it another go?" he said.

People were zipping past us. Some were as confident about it as he had been when I first saw him, weaving in and out of the throng with calm faces. Others were more like me, going so tentatively that their skates were barely engaging with the ice. There were groups of kids on the loose, kids with parents, a few older people like me, and even an elderly man with white hair who was looping his way around the rink with an air of utter absorption.

I was already here. I'd already made a prat out of myself. The damp patch of melted ice on my arse and the dull throbbing in my elbows bore testament to that. Everyone around me was smiling and pink-cheeked. Why not attempt to join them?

He nudged me gently. "Yes?"

I stopped clinging to the barrier and wobbled to a (mostly) upright position. "Yes," I said.

"All right! That's what I like to hear. Now, before you—oh, shit."

I took one step, my legs went out from under me, and my kneecaps hit the ice with a sound like fucking walnuts being cracked at Christmas.

He shoved his hands under my arms, and hauled me up again.

I was so surprised at how easily he moved me about, I went as limp as a ragdoll cat.

He propped me against the barrier. "Try it again, but this time, keep in contact with the ice." He pointed at himself and demonstrated a graceful, easy start.

Right. Don't pick your foot up like you're walking. Got it.

Honestly, I could have watched at least *one* tutorial on YouTube before I left the house.

He swivelled around to face me with a fluid twist of his hips, and held out his hands expectantly.

He did it with such confidence, I put my hands in his without even questioning it. He closed his fingers around mine, and squeezed gently. "I'm Jakub, by the way. Jake."

"Ben."

"Okay, Ben. Let's go. Just like I showed you. It's easy as—oh, shit."

He caught me before my knees hit the ice a second time.

Unfortunately, only just.

In other words, I was now dangling from the hands he'd wedged under my arms, I had my nose pressed to his abs a scant inch above the waistband of his tight grey sweatpants, and my dick was being stupid about it.

Of course my dick was being stupid about it.

He smelled *divine*. Laundry detergent, a woodsy body wash, and clean, warm man.

For god's sake. I mentally smacked myself.

I clutched his hips and made the mistake of looking up and meeting his eyes.

He was laughing at me.

My face went so hot, I was astonished I didn't bore a hole straight through the ice and down into the bowels of Hell.

To whence I would like to consign this whole day, frankly.

He stopped laughing and made a soft noise as he hauled me up. "I'm not laughing *at* you," he said. "I'm laughing *with* you."

I straightened my spine and pushed his hands off me, avoiding his gaze. "I wouldn't blame you if you were laughing at me. I'm being ridiculous. This whole idea was ridiculous. I don't know what I was thinking."

I should have stayed at home and sulked.

"Ben. Hey." He tapped my shoulder, making me look at him. "You're not being ridiculous. You're having a good time."

"Usually when I'm having a good time, I smile more."

"Then let's see if we can make you smile more. Come on, try again. You're good at this remember?"

"I *was* good," I said, aggrieved. "I really was! I don't know what's going on. Actually, yes I do. I think it's the skates."

"The skates?"

"Yes. Last time I came, I had the kind of skates that lace up. These ones are made out of plastic. They've got clips, like ski boots."

"Ah." He nodded. "That's probably it, then."

"You think?"

"Yep. We can solve that, easy." He grabbed my hands, scooted me backwards, ignoring my yelp as I clutched at him, and turned me around. He crowded behind me, propelled us to the exit, and manoeuvred me off the ice and onto solid ground.

Hallelujah.

"This way," he said, and herded me from the rink to the benches and lockers close to the skate rental counter, where he sat me down.

I stared at him, wide-eyed, as he went to his knees before me.

What the—

Oh.

He unsnapped my right skate with a practiced flick of his thumb, and patted my calf. "Up."

I did as I was told, and was quickly stripped of first the right and then the left skate.

"Stay right there," he said, standing to his full height, which was even more impressive from where I sat. "I'll be right back. Okay?"

"O-kay." My throat clicked.

He paused to grin at me before he stalked off to the counter, approximately ten feet tall with the extra lift from his skates.

There wasn't much of a queue, what with the public session being in full swing by now, but there were a couple of people waiting. For a horrified moment, I thought he was going to shove his way to the front and demand a new pair. Instead, he opened the door next to the hatch marked STAFF, let himself in, and vanished from sight.

I really hoped that he worked here.

Folding at the waist, I laid my forearms along my thighs, letting my hands dangle.

What the fuck was I even doing?

I was getting all hot and bothered over the sexy, athletic young thing taking pity on my incompetent, middle-aged arse, going above and beyond his job description, and being *nice* about it. That's what I was doing.

That poor boy had *no idea* that, while he was helping

with my skates, I was sitting here, thinking about those hard abs I'd had my face squashed against, about those ridiculously long legs, the truly phenomenal arse I'd goggled at as he strutted ahead of me, and most of all, about the kindness in his strong hands and the patience in his pretty eyes.

I let the sounds of happy people and shouting kids wash over me as I waited for him to return.

It didn't take long. Not two minutes later, Jake reappeared with a new pair of boots. His gaze arrowed straight to the bench where he'd left me sitting in my socks. The faint frown on his face vanished as soon as he saw me.

He stalked over and, once again, went to his knees before me.

I was almost sure I'd kept my lecherous and inappropriate thoughts off my face, going on the bright smile I received when he glanced up at me, before he grabbed my ankle and lifted my socked foot.

I swayed backwards, tipped off balance, and heard a dull thud as my phone fell out of my pocket and bounced off the bench to the floor.

Keeping hold of my ankle, Jake swiped the phone up and handed it to me. I murmured my thanks and stuffed it back in my pocket, making a mental note to wear baggier jeans if I decided to give skating another go. Right now, I was on the fence.

"Try this," he said, slipping my foot into the boot.

It was another cheap blue plastic rental skate.

"They didn't have any of the good ones available?" I said, not hiding my disappointment well. Or at all.

"These are the only ones they hire out. You want the good ones, you have to buy a pair and bring them."

"How much will that set me back?"

"About fifty pounds for a basic pair, a hundred for a decent pair."

That wasn't too bad, and it was a one-off payment. My rarely used gym membership was currently sucking forty quid a month out of my bank account. Maybe, if I got back into this, I'd treat myself. Freeze the gym membership, buy some good skates. Come back here. See him again…

Jake braced my leg and snapped the clips closed. "How does that feel?"

I had enough room to wiggle my toes and the boot didn't pinch, except for where it pressed down on the top of my foot. I always had that problem with shoes and boots. I got the high arches from my mother.

"Feels pretty good," I said.

"Yeah?"

I nodded.

"All right." He gave my other calf a light smack. "Now this one."

Again, I lifted my foot and watched while he tucked it into the boot for me.

It wasn't until the press of his thumb in a sensitive spot made me suck in a startled breath that I suddenly thought, hang on a minute. What's going on here?

There was being helpful, and there was this: Jake, on his knees, putting my skates on for me.

That wasn't normal.

…was it?

Maybe I wasn't the only one having inappropriate thoughts here.

Maybe Jake was having some inappropriate thoughts of his own.

This time when he looked up at me expectantly, there was a little…?

Was there?

...*was* there a little something in his eyes?

We stared at each other for a long, charged moment.

"Well?" he said.

"Well?"

He wrapped his big hands around both my calves and shook my legs cheerfully. My thighs wobbled. Okay, that wasn't sexy. "How does that one feel?"

"Uh. Kind of the same as the other one."

"Comfortable?" he checked.

I wiggled my toes again. "Yes."

"This should make all the difference. Ready to go and give them a try?"

He stood up, slowly and from his position right between my legs, giving me plenty of time to absorb the delicious unfolding of his tall body. He flashed me another smile and tipped his head in the direction of the ice. "If you want to do this, Ben, let's go."

I pushed up off the bench and tested my balance. They *did* feel better. After another long stare, Jake gave a challenging lift of his chin and strode off. Like a duckling, I waddled after him, and he hauled me straight onto the ice.

He scooped an arm around my waist, turned me, and skated me backwards until we were clear of the gate. The manoeuvre also happened to put us chest to chest, which I wasn't mad about.

All of this before I had a chance to catch my breath or protest.

He propped me against the barrier and gave me some personal space.

Not a whole lot, I couldn't help but notice.

"Sorry about that," he said. "It's easier for the general flow to move away from the gate as soon as possible."

Once again, Jake held out his hands to me, this time at waist height. He opened and closed his fingers in unspoken demand.

Once again, I took them without question—I *had* to stop doing things just because a gorgeous stranger told me to—and let him rearrange the grip so that I was holding onto his thick forearms instead. Muscle flexed beneath my palms.

"Get a feel for it," he said. "Ben?"

"Huh?" I dragged my gaze off his flexing forearms.

He moved his skates forwards and backwards, then held in place and bounced up and down lightly. "Feel your connection to the ice. Settle your centre of gravity nice and low. Don't be afraid to bend your legs a lot more than you think you need to. Wiggle around a bit. I won't let you fall."

"Good luck trying to stop me."

"I'm doing all right so far."

"You are, thank you."

He squeezed.

I dropped my weight down into the blades and shuffled my feet cautiously. "Wow. These skates are seriously so much better! Who knew!"

"It's just a matter of finding the right pair for you. Ready to go?"

"Yes!" I said with enthusiasm. And then, when he let go, "No!" with equal enthusiasm.

He laughed. "Come on. Like this. You can do it." He stood beside me, and pushed off gently.

Fine. I had to try. I did, after all, come here to skate, not to cling to a beautiful man and let him do all the work.

Although, clinging to a beautiful man and letting him do all the work *was* one of my very favourite things to do.

Just not in a public forum.

I pushed off, braced for impact, and...did not fall over.

"You've got it," Jake said with an encouraging nod. "Now keep going."

I dug in, pushed off, glided forwards. Shifted my weight into my left foot, did it again...right foot...left... "Hah!" I said. "I told you I was good at skating!"

"Yep." His eyes sparkled at me when I turned to look up at him in triumph, and widened when I tripped.

I groaned and sat up on my aching butt. "That was your fault," I said.

"How was it my fault?" He crouched down, snagged me, and dragged me back up, all in one uninterrupted and well-practiced movement.

You sparkled at me and felled me with your sexiness. "You made me look up. Totally compromised my balance."

"In that case, I can only apologise."

"Forgiven," I said loftily, then yelped and grabbed for him when he pushed me backwards. "*What are you doing?*"

"Getting you used to the feel of the ice."

"Backwards, though?"

"Feel the ice, Ben. Don't think about it, relax into it. I've got you."

I stopped watching my feet and met his eyes instead.

I've got you.

My heart skipped.

"All right," I said.

3

He picked up speed and I laughed, high and breathless. I softened into his embrace and went with it.

It was *wonderful*.

"Take me around again," I demanded once we'd done a full circuit.

He obligingly did.

This.

This was what I'd been searching for when I came up with my stupid idea.

This feeling, right here. Freedom. Happiness. Being one hundred percent in the moment, something I'd struggled to do my whole life.

I was beaming as we completed the second circuit and came to a gentle stop.

"Did you like that?" Jake said, even though it was more than obvious that I did.

"Yes! It's exactly what I needed today. What I came here for. Thank you."

"Good, and you're welcome."

I released his arms. He held on a second longer before letting go.

"Ready to try it on your own?" he said.

"Yes," I said, and struck off cautiously.

He followed, gliding along beside me, keeping me tucked between the barrier and his body.

We skated in comfortable silence for a full circuit, and then continued around for another.

"I really do appreciate this," I said, risking my balance to sneak a quick glance up at him. He was watching me with a faint smile on his lips. "I was about to give up. If you hadn't shown up, I'd have crawled off the ice, gone home, and done my best to erase the memory."

And never, ever, told anyone about it.

Ever.

"Happy to help." He turned his hips with a fluid twist and skated backwards a foot ahead of me.

"So, what's your job title here?" I asked. "I want to get it right for when I give you a shoutout in my five star review on Trip Advisor."

He looked at me blankly.

"Sorry. That was a joke. I don't leave reviews. I am curious, though. Are you an ice…steward? Or something? Ice… host? Ice marshal?"

"I don't work for the rink. I work here independently. I'm a coach."

"You're a coach? Are you…are you coaching me right now? Because I didn't pay for a coach! I paid for the public skate. This isn't a case of mistaken identity is it?"

I'd poached someone's coach. That was worse than sitting in someone else's reserved seat on the train.

"No. I have a class to teach when the public session ends in a bit, and I like to warm up on my own first. Ben, I didn't come over and pick you up because I mistakenly thought you were a new client."

"Oh." I sagged. What a relief.

"I came over to help. I don't like to see people struggling and in all my years skating, I've never seen anyone struggle quite like you. You fell over three times in three minutes."

"Tell me something I don't know." My arse was still complaining about it.

"All right. I didn't come over just to help. I was thinking that maybe I could get your number. Oh, shit."

I groaned and sat up.

"You okay?" he asked.

"Yes." *Seriously*, my arse. I was going to have to swing by the pharmacy on the way home and pick up some arnica cream and ibuprofen.

I waited expectantly, but Jake just stood there, hands on hips, looking down at me.

I tipped my head back. "A little help?"

He smiled slowly. "I think you'd better do it on your own this time."

I scowled. "Or we could skip the part where I flop around like a pillock, and you could get me up?"

"Nope," he said with a cheerful shake of his head. "If I actually was your coach, we'd have started with this. Come on. You know what I want you to do. Get on your hands and knees for me."

He gave me that innocent look again.

I wasn't fooled.

I bit my lip to hide my smile and did as he said, feeling weird about getting on all fours at his feet as he towered over me now that I knew he was interested, but not *hating* it.

"What now?" I said.

"I want you to push up so you're on one knee with the

other leg bent in front of you, brace your hands on your bent thigh, and then push all the way up to standing. Don't overthink it."

I overthought everything.

"You can do it," he said.

I blew out a breath and did as he said, going from hands and knees to kneeling.

I got one leg out in front of me, my skate shot over the ice, and I folded into an involuntary hamstring stretch, nose almost hitting my outstretched leg. "Ahhh. Oh, no. I think I pulled my groin."

"Uh-huh," he said, hooking his hands under my arms and scooping me up with another display of strength that hit me right in the gut. "You're not being lazy and making me do it for you or anything."

Fine, maybe I'd sort of leant into it unnecessarily when my blade skittered out from under me, but I wasn't here to learn how to get up off the ice, I wanted to learn how to not fall in the first place.

And I told him so.

"Can't do one without the other," he said, a hand low at my back to propel me forwards. I went easily. "That's good, Ben. Great balance. You're improving."

"Thanks!" I was gaining confidence with every passing minute. While I was nowhere near the hotshot I remembered being, I wasn't doing too badly at all.

I was also on the fast track to developing a praise kink.

Whenever he said *good* like that, I felt the word resonate somewhere deep inside in a way it certainly hadn't when my mother had said it earlier today.

And maybe I had a competence kink, too. I did admire a man who knew what the fuck he was doing.

Or maybe it was simply him.

I *liked* him.

He skated along beside me in silence for a few strokes, then held out his hand. I took it without thinking. He folded his fingers around mine, warm and firm.

It was lovely, right up until he said, "I'm going to turn you, okay?"

"*Turn* me? What do you—no, wait, I—ahhh!"

He drew me into his arms and turned me, swinging us around in an easy circle. My upper body snapped forwards and backwards suddenly, but I managed to keep my feet.

"Good," he said.

Good.

My stomach tightened. Yeah, I was in trouble.

"Let's do it again."

"Jake! I—*ahhh!*"

I screeched then laughed, loud and happy. Jake's grin faded but his amusement lingered. As did the warmth in his eyes.

This time when he turned us, once I was facing the right way, he let me go and stuffed his hands in his pockets. He skated backwards in front of me. "Keep looking at me. You're doing great."

I'd realised that while he was distracting me with the turns and the sparkle in his eyes and that beautiful smile on his beautiful face, I'd somehow slipped back into the rhythm of skating, making long, easy strokes over the ice. I didn't even falter when I jittered over the deep gouges and ridges left by all the other skaters who'd been around since the ice was last Zamboni-ed.

It helped that the blades were sharper than on my first pair.

"Thank you for sorting my skates out," I said. "It's amazing the difference the right pair makes."

Jake's smile bloomed wider.

"What?" I said suspiciously.

"It's all you, Ben," he said.

I wanted to preen a bit at this confirmation that I *was*, as I had suspected all along, a natural, but while I could—and would—wilfully delude myself about many things, my arse, elbows and kneecaps were insisting I wasn't remotely a natural. I was inclined to believe them.

"What does that mean, exactly? It's all me?"

"It means they're the same skates."

I stared. "What?" I said after an indignant pause.

"They are the same skates."

"You…? You tricked me?"

"*You* were tricking you. Telling yourself you couldn't do it."

"So you, what? You took them away, counted to sixty, and brought them back out to me?"

"One hundred and twenty," he said.

"Huh?"

"I counted to one hundred and twenty. Two minutes. Thought you'd get suspicious if I was too quick about it."

I glared at him. "You sharpened them, though? They're not the exact same?"

"Nope. They are the exact same skates."

I glared some more. "How did you know there was nothing wrong with them?"

"Two reasons. One, I'm a professional. I checked them out, and they're fine. They're shit because they're rentals but other than that, they're fine. And two, most people who have skated a few times before, even if it was a long time ago, can pick it back up well enough to at least stay upright within a few minutes. You just went straight out. It's a mind game."

"You know it all, huh?"

"I do," he agreed mildly. "When it comes to skating, anyway. Look at you go."

I was skating easily, freely, swinging my arms and chasing after him as he hip-swivelled his taunting way ahead of me.

"It's my job," he said. "This is what I do. I'm a coach. I've even got some fancy sports psychology qualifications. I know what it takes to compete, what makes you fail, what gives you the edge."

"Yeah? Did you ever compete yourself?"

He ducked his head. "I did."

"Here in the UK, or in Europe?"

"All over the world."

"Really? Did you keep getting traded? I always thought that must be tough."

He sighed. "I didn't play hockey, if that's what you're thinking."

It was what I was thinking. "No?"

He'd be a formidable sight in hockey gear, powering up the ice, putting the fear of God into the goalie.

Hockey wasn't a big thing in the UK, not like in the rest of Europe and the US, but it *was* a thing. I was aware of it.

"Nope. I was a figure skater."

I couldn't help it. I checked him out, head to toe and back again, imagining the spandex and the sequins.

I swallowed hard.

If I'd thought that Jake would be an impressive sight in hockey gear, then the idea of him in skintight clothing with a bit of sparkle, some ruffles or feathers…well, it was a very different lens to view him through, and not a bad one.

At all.

What in the name of all that was holy did his arse look

like, bouncing around in Lycra? People in the audience would faint at the sight of it, surely?

I knew I would.

"Were you any good?" I croaked.

"Not bad," he said with a breezy shrug.

Too breezy. "How not bad?"

He just smiled.

I eyed him. "Out of ten, how not bad?"

"That's not how the ISU scoring system works."

I had no idea who or what the ISU was. "Pretend it is. On a scale of one to ten? What would you be?"

Another of those breezy shrugs. "I'd be a nine point five."

"Can't imagine why someone wouldn't give you a ten."

He slowed his pace so that I caught up to him, then slid an arm around my waist. I did another involuntary vertical jackknife and overcompensated in the opposite direction, but I managed to stay upright.

Okay, Jake managed to keep me upright.

"That's sweet of you," he said.

My hands rested on his chest as he lazily turned us and wove around the ice, never even getting close to colliding with anyone. I softened in his arms and let it happen.

"Were you a solo skater? Is that the right way to say it? I don't know the proper term, sorry. Or were you a pair?"

"I competed single and with a partner. I was good at both, but I always preferred a partner." His eyes gleamed at me.

"Did you win any competitions?"

He nodded, his cheeks dusted with colour. "One or two."

That was way too modest.

"You won medals, didn't you?" I asked.

He bit his lip. "One or two."

"What kind of medal?" He'd said he competed all over the world. "Not the Olympics?"

He shrugged.

I gasped theatrically. "Am I really being taught how to skate by an Olympic medallist?"

"Maybe."

"I thought everyone was staring at me because I was with the hottest guy on the ice, not because I was with a *celebrity*. I did *not* see this coming for my birthday."

His arm flexed when I called him the hottest guy, and he drew us closer together. "It's your birthday?" he said.

"You're an Olympian?" I deflected. "Tell me more."

"Yes, I was. A long time ago. In another life. But it's your birthday? Today?"

"Ugh. Yes."

"Happy birthday! How old are you?"

I froze, and we nearly went down. Jake gave a soft laugh as he executed some fancy footwork to keep us upright. Loosening his grip, he swung back to skate alongside me instead of turning us in our lazy, waltzing loops.

"Would you believe I'm twenty-one?" I asked.

His gaze tracked up to the *slight* scattering of grey at my temples. He didn't say anything. He didn't have to.

I scowled. "How about thirty-one? Would you believe that?"

He squeezed my hand. "You're one of those people who get dramatic about birthdays, aren't you?"

I gasped again. "Me?"

"I'm guessing thirty-five," he said.

I beamed.

He snorted. "That means older than thirty-five."

Well, I gave that one away. "I'm forty."

"Huh."

My heart sank and I shot him a cautious look from the corner of my eye.

"You make forty look good," he said.

I couldn't hide my stupid smile. "So, uh. How about you? How old are you?"

"Guess."

I scanned him and sighed. "Twenty-five?" I said.

"You're out by more than a decade. Thirty-seven."

"You're thirty-seven?" I'd thought he was *younger* than twenty-five. I'd tacked on a couple of years in a feeble attempt to make myself feel less like an old creep.

How could he be thirty-seven?

His fair skin was unlined and unwrinkled, apart from the faint creases by his eyes when he smiled. He was exuding rude health. *Rude*. Then again, he was a professional athlete. Kind of his job to be in peak physical form, I supposed. And since ice skating was an indoor sport, the sun had a hard time getting at him to turn him into a raisin like the rest of us.

"Yep," he said. "Thirty-seven. Which is why my professional career is long over. Although, I stopped competing less because of my age and more because of my size."

I gave him another, thorough, head to toe. "Is it not an advantage?" I thought it would be. Six-two, six-three. Wide shoulders, big arms, the aforementioned amazing arse, and let's not forget the quads straining at his sweatpants.

He could lift a tiny little partner in each hand.

Forget pairs, he could do throuple figure skating.

"Not beyond a certain point, no," he said. "Most male skaters are under six foot. I was still growing when I retired at twenty."

"That's a shame. Do you miss it?"

"Yeah. It's kind of the downside of any competitive career, though, not just figure skating. You're on a clock from the second you start. The end is always coming at you, one way or the other. Either you finish early because of an injury, or you retire because you're too old for it."

Not unlike life. "That's a bit bleak."

"Ice skating isn't all sequins and ruffles."

I scanned him again.

He smiled slowly. "You're imagining me in sequins and ruffles, aren't you, Ben?"

Why lie? "Yes, I am. I'd like to see that some time. If I went onto YouTube and typed in *Jake the Olympic Figure Skater*, could I find some videos of you in all your fancy finery, busting a few medal-winning moves?"

"Yes. Or you could ask for a private performance."

I gaped up at him.

He snorted a laugh. "Before you get too excited, it wouldn't be in costume. I couldn't fit into any of my costumes now. I was built a lot leaner back then."

"Still think you'd look pretty good," I said.

"Why, thank you, Ben." He flipped around and skated backwards.

"Let's see one of your fancy moves, then."

He raised an eyebrow.

"Hey, you were the one who brought up a private performance, not me," I said.

"All right." He guided us to a stop by the barrier and pushed me backwards gently until my arse bumped into it. He shuffled closer and stared down at me, his body heat warming me through. "Try not to be too overcome with admiration."

"I'll do my best."

The rink was significantly emptier than it had been earlier. I'd lost track of time completely.

Giving me a cocky grin, Jake shot backwards, going from stationary to top speed with zero apparent effort, and stopped dramatically in the open ice at the centre of the rink.

He held his long arms wide open, as if he was gathering, no, *demanding* attention, and the grace in his big body was astounding. I'd already noticed it, but now he was in performance mode it was deliberate, focused, turned all the way up.

And then he turned it up even higher, exploding into action.

He was absolutely mesmerising.

Jake didn't glide over the ice, he struck out over it like he owned every last inch of it.

He powered over it, claiming it.

He was wearing close-fitting, forest-green sweatpants—not quite leggings—and they stretched tight over his quads and his arse as he moved. To my horror, I made an inappropriate wanting noise and had to cover with a gruff and incredibly fake cough, in case there was anyone close enough to hear me.

There could have been a thousand people right there, or we could have been the only two left on the rink. I only had eyes for Jake.

He scored over the ice, whooshed past me close enough that I felt the rush of his speed over my exposed skin, ruffling my hair, and turned backwards. He gathered himself, drew in tight, and leapt into the air, turning with his arms tucked in close, and landed on one freaking leg, and... well. Sigh.

What a spectacular sight.

I leaned against the barrier right where he'd put me, and watched wide-eyed as Jake really showed me his stuff. Big, looping circles. Quick direction changes, leaps and spins. On one leg, on two legs.

I was surprised he didn't stand on his head.

If he wanted to, he probably could.

He pushed into one last, insanely fast turn, whipping around on the spot, then stopped and opened his arms out as wide as when he'd started, head dropped back to gaze artistically up at the rafters, long body arched. He held for a final, throbbing moment (well, I was throbbing, I didn't know about him. His sweatpants were tight but not that tight) and then relaxed.

Hands in his pockets, crossing his skates casually one in front of the other, he sauntered over the ice, eyes on me, and came to a stop way too close.

Or not close enough. If I had my way, he'd have slid all the way up into my personal space until we were bumping chests again. He'd have been able to feel how damn fast my heart was beating, and I'd have been able to feel his.

I stared up at him. "Wow," I croaked.

"Yeah?" He grinned, cheeks rosy. I'd thought he ran hot before, but the heat pouring off his body now was incredible.

I nodded. "That was amazing. I mean. Wow. Especially that bit just before the end. The jump? Double wow."

"Triple Axel," he said, "but close."

I swallowed, still staring up at him. "Are you sure you didn't retire too early? Not to pump your tires or anything, but that looked world class to me. I feel like I should be throwing flowers at you. Isn't that what people do?"

"Sometimes."

I mimed it.

I *mimed* it.

Shit.

"That was...I...me throwing flowers."

"Ah."

Aaaaand like the absolute pillock that I was, because my joke hadn't landed, I decided to double down. "And here's the medal."

I mimed hanging it around his neck.

Back when I was a teenager, I'd spent many a moody hour lying on my bed, grumping up at the ceiling, sighing heavily at the *trials* of my *life* and waiting impatiently for the future to arrive.

Because in the future I'd have learned how to be a proper human being, I wouldn't be such a fucking nerd, and I wouldn't always act like a total idiot in front of cute boys.

And for sure when I was a proper oldie, like thirty or the horrifying and unimaginable *forty*, I'd be so far over the awkward embarrass-yourself-in-public stage that I wouldn't even remember that time in life.

Right?

Sorry, Teenage Me.

Hard no.

I was going to keep making new and embarrassing memories until the day I died.

"That's weird," I said to Jake. "Forget I did it."

He was smiling at me, a little bemused, with one side of his lips tipped up. His eyes were warm. He twisted his hips from side to side in that way he had, swaying a few inches this way, a few inches that. "I think I like weird." He looked down at the *invisible* fucking medal I'd just hung around his neck, patted his chest right over where it would hang, and said, quite seriously, "This is a gold, right?"

"Eh. You were good, but you were a bit shaky on a couple of the landings, so—"

He gripped my hips and tugged me into him quickly, pressing us together. "It's a gold."

"Yes. Congratulations. Gold for Great Britain."

"Oh, no," he shook his head slowly. "Jakub Kowalczyk. I'm only half-British. I skated for Poland."

"My apologies. Gold for Poland!" I held up my hands and raised the roof.

Holy crap.

Was I trying to win gold in *embarrassing myself*? Because if I didn't get my shit under control, I had a good chance of succeeding.

Jake's smile faded but the warmth on his face remained. "Ben?"

"Yeah?"

"Do you have anything else planned for your birthday?"

"Nothing that can top a private coaching session and then an impromptu performance from an Olympian figure skater." He waited. "Oh. No? I've got my gym bag in the car but let's not fool ourselves here. I will not go. I'll do my weekly shop and run some errands, but other than that I'll just head home and hang out. Chill." Have another panic about getting older, cry into a bottle of rosé Prosecco, and then get over it until my fiftieth birthday rolled around. "Nothing too exciting."

"Would you like to go to dinner instead? With me?"

"Yes," I said straight away. Goddammit, I practically choked, I answered so quickly. "Yes. I'd like that."

"And perhaps I can give you a birthday kiss?"

He could give me a birthday *anything*. "That sounds—oh."

First Dates and Birthday Cakes | 47

He did it. Right there.

He lowered his head and dropped a firm, warm kiss on my lips.

"I didn't think you meant now," I said, once he'd pulled back and we'd stared at each other in silence.

Jake looked surprised, his eyes dark and pupils wide. "I didn't," he said. "I meant after dinner. Couldn't help it. Sorry."

"No, no. Don't apologise. You can do it again, if you like."

"I will." His attention dropped to my lips and his chest expanded in a deep breath. "But I'll have to wait until later. Public skate's over and I've got to get to work." He held me against him for another long moment, then reluctantly glided back a respectable few inches.

My surroundings swung back into focus. The crowd had dwindled to a mere handful of people. At the other end of the rink, the Zamboni trundled into view, getting ready to resurface the ice.

"Grab your phone and I'll give you my number," Jake said, one eye on the small group of loudly chattering people coming from the locker area.

I added him as a contact and sent him a text.

He knew a great restaurant, he said, and would make the booking, and text me the time and place when he'd finished work.

And that was it.

He whisked me to the gate—*in case you fall over again*—squeezed my hip gently, and skated off.

Well, I thought as I clomped towards the benches by the rental counter, this whole outing had worked out *very* differently from how I'd envisaged it.

I turned and looked over my shoulder at the rink, where

Jake was standing in front of the people who'd flocked to him over the ice.

Instead of rekindling the innocent, optimistic *joie de vivre* of my extreme youth, I seemed to have snagged myself a date with a hot, interesting, *nice* guy.

I'd had worse birthdays.

4
───────

I'd had worse birthdays, it was true.

And this one could very well turn out to be the worst of the lot.

I stood on my doorstep, my key frozen in mid-air, and stared up at Ravi's face in horror.

Behind him, an enormous banner stretched across my hall, proclaiming in foot-high, powder-blue letters against a scorching-pink background, *HAPPY BIRTHDAY, BABY BOY!!!*

There were balloons.

There were streamers.

He was wearing a sparkly rainbow party hat.

"You didn't," I groaned.

"Fuck yeah, I did. Woo!" Ravi opened the front door wider and hauled me through.

Two people burst out of my utility closet, the kitchen door whacked open at the other end of the hall to reveal my beaming parents, and three other people got wedged in the doorway to the sitting room when they all tried to run out at once. Dad did his thing with a party popper again, making my mother screech.

Everyone yelled, "Happy Birthday!"

I smiled, even as I said through gritted teeth, "*Ravi.*"

He slouched in the doorway, his black hair in its usual tousled mess under the stupid hat and his dark eyes shining with mischief. "Let's party, bitch."

"Actually—"

"Haha. Fuck no. There is no 'actually'. You are partying. You're forty, Ben. *Forty*! Life starts now! With a party."

He snatched my gym bag off me and tossed it in the direction of my console table, then stripped me out of my coat with alarming efficiency and slung it on the coatrack. While I was saying things like, "My groceries are in the car," and, "My ice cream's melting," and, "Why aren't my parents in Scotland?" he fussed with my hair, took the hat off his head and stuck it on mine, turned me by the shoulders, and shoved me into the sitting room ahead of him.

He'd really gone all out.

There were even more balloons and streamers in here than in the hall, and even more people.

Eighties music played, platters of Waitrose's finest party food covered every flat surface, and to top it off, my coffee table was all but buckling under the weight of a spectacularly huge birthday cake.

"This is terrible timing," I hissed at Ravi.

"You want to talk about terrible timing? Where the hell have you been all day? You were supposed to be at home, brooding. I had a plan. Your mum was going to surprise you first, lure you out for the afternoon and keep you clear of the house while I set up for the real surprise, but you weren't here and you weren't answering your damn phone. We had to wing it. Lizzie sat in her car watching the top of your road for an hour to give us a heads-up. Sitting in her car is not

Lizzie's idea of a good time on a Saturday afternoon. I am going to have to service her like you wouldn't believe to say thank you."

"Ravi, no. Don't tell me about your sex life."

He ignored me. "Everyone gather around," he yelled, clapping his hands for attention, then shooting finger guns at the cake. "You've all been drooling long enough while we waited and waited and *waited* for Ben to get his arse home. Let's carve this motherfucker *up*."

"I really do have a date," I said behind him as the crowd of friends, family, and friendly coworkers surged towards the coffee table.

"Okay, hold your forks, people," Ravi yelled. "Keep mingling. Go nuts with the buffet. No one touch that cake. We'll be back in a mo."

He scruffed me and towed me out into the hall. He ran me clear through the house, whisking me through the kitchen and all the way out the back door.

Once outside, he pushed me against the wall. "A date? Really? You haven't had a date in five years, and you chose *today* to break your dry spell?"

"I'm as surprised as you are, to be honest."

That was a lie. I was way more surprised.

"Right, well. You're not getting out of your own party, so forget it. You will go in there and you will enjoy yourself—or pretend you are enjoying yourself—if I have to shove my hand up your arse and make you my muppet. I'm a trauma surgeon, and I've done much, much worse."

I knew he had. I'd heard the stories. "I don't want to be your muppet."

More importantly, Ravi had gone to a massive amount of effort to spring this nightmare upon my unsuspecting head, and I was truly touched. I wouldn't have to pretend anything.

"Call your guy and tell him there's been a change of plans," Ravi said. "Have him come along. I'm sure he'd love to meet a bunch of strangers on a first date, including family members of the guy he's trying to shag and everyone knows it. Who wouldn't?"

You'd think that Ravi was being sarcastic, but he wasn't. Crashing someone's surprise birthday party was his idea of a fantastic time.

"Brilliant," I said. "*Yes*. You're a genius."

"I know."

I'd enjoy the party, I'd get to see Jake, and I'd…I patted my pocket. "Hang on. Where's my fucking phone?"

"I'm guessing it's not in your pocket?" Ravi said.

"*No!*"

"Is it in your coat, maybe? Gym bag?"

"No, I always…in my back pocket…"

"I've told you a hundred times not to put it in your back pocket, or to at least size up your jeans. There isn't enough room for your arse *and* your phone."

"It's convenient, and I like my jeans snug!"

"Not convenient right now, is it? It wasn't convenient when you dropped it down the can, either. Twice."

"You're not helping," I said over my shoulder as I rushed back inside. I barrelled through the kitchen and into the hall, glancing through the sitting room doorway en route.

As Ravi had ordered, people were mingling, and people had hit the buffet. People had point-blank ignored the order about the cake, though, because it had been sliced and loaded onto an elegantly arranged fan of plates. My mother was the one holding the knife and handing it out.

I snatched my coat off the coatrack and gave it a thorough shakedown. Nope. Nothing. Fine. No need to panic.

Gym bag.

I dropped the coat to the floor, hit my sore knees, and unzipped my gym bag. I scuffled through it, then lost all sense of decorum and upended it, scattering the contents to the parquet floor and pawing through it all frantically.

No phone.

I sat back on my heels and dropped my chin to my chest.

"Listen," Ravi said, putting a hand on my shoulder. "This isn't the end of the world." He crouched beside me and started scooping things back up and stuffing them into the gym bag.

"It *is* the end of the world. I had a *date* planned, Ravi," I said. "Do you know how long it's been since I had a date?"

He grabbed my coat, he grabbed my arm, and he stood, dragging me up with him. "Five years. We just covered that. Keep up."

"Five years! And Jake is so nice! He's the nicest guy I've ever met, and now I'm going to be the worst guy he's ever met, because he'll be sitting there all alone at the restaurant, waiting for me to show, and I won't show! Because I don't know which restaurant to show at! *Because I don't have my phone.*"

"We can find it. Think. Where were you and what were you doing the last time you remember having it? At the supermarket? Petrol station? In the car?"

Oh. "The ice rink."

Ravi blinked. "The what now?"

"The ice rink. That's when I last remember having it."

I'd entered Jake's contact details and sent him a text, and then done exactly as I'd told him I would—avoided the gym, went to the supermarket, ran a couple of errands, and headed home.

"Ben?" Ravi said. "I have to ask. What the fuck were you doing at the ice rink?"

I huffed. "I was sort of...I was depressed this morning, okay?"

"Uh-huh. And you thought, *I know how to fix this. I'll take myself ice skating*?"

"It's not the weirdest thing in the world," I said.

"It's not the most normal, either."

"I was being punk."

"By ice skating."

"Yes."

"...okay, I'm not sure how that works. Doesn't matter. Moving on...if the last time you remember having it is at the ice rink, then odds are, that's where it is."

"Ugh. When I don't show up for our date or reply to his texts, Jake is going to think I'm ghosting him."

"Yeah, he is," Ravi said. "But only for a while. Tomorrow, you'll go and see if your phone is at the ice rink, which I'm sure it is, you'll call him and explain, problem solved."

"You make it sound so easy."

"It is easy. Your phone will still be there tomorrow. This Jake guy will laugh about it when you explain, and if he doesn't, then he's a humourless bastard and you're better off without him."

"I suppose."

"Or..." Ravi said thoughtfully.

I perked up. "Or?" I liked the sound of *or*.

He took out his own phone—front pocket—poked at it a few times, and lifted it to his ear. "I'm calling you," he said. "If it's at the rink and someone turned it in, they'll have it at reception. Maybe I can charm them into bringing your phone here. When I say charm, I do of course mean bribe. You're still not sneaking out of this party to meet him, but you can text or call him tonight. That way, he won't have to cry himself to sleep, thinking the hot forty-something weirdo ghosted him. Oh. Hey, someone picked up. Hello?"

"Give me that." I lunged at him. He held me back with a hand at the centre of my chest.

"Who is *this*? Oh? *Really*?" Ravi winked at me. "Hello, *Jake*. I didn't see that one coming. I'm Ravi, and I'm calling about Ben's phone."

"Give me the phone," I said and made another grab for it. Ravi ducked me again.

"Listen, Jake. I heard you were supposed to be going on a date tonight. Mm-hmm. Yeah. Thing is, Ben won't be able to make it. What? No, no. Nothing like that. I mean, he's sexy as hell, but I just don't see him that way. He has a prior engagement he didn't know about. As in, I threw the ungrateful bastard a surprise birthday party, and we have cake and champagne and I think you'll agree it would be pretty rude of him to go running off to meet some guy for a hookup and —Oh? *Not* a hookup? A date? I'm sorry, a *first* date? That's good to know. Because my boy isn't really a hookup kind of guy."

"I mean it, Ravi—"

"So how about you come over here and have yourself a piece of cake?"

"What?" I said loudly.

Ravi looked at me and rolled his eyes. "Would you hold on a moment while I check with him to see if he's okay with you knowing where he lives?"

"You can't say that," I hissed.

"Just did. Want him to come over or not?"

I stared. "Yes?"

"Jake, he doesn't sound too sure about it, so—*oh my god*, you bitch." Ravi doubled over laughing when I got him in the side with a hard tickle.

I snatched the phone off him. "I'll take it from here," I said. "Thank you."

"You're welcome. Tell him to hurry up. I'll do my best to save him some cake but you have a bunch of jackals in your sitting room and I can't make promises." He raised his voice. "Bye, Jake!" he called, and swaggered off.

I held the phone to my ear, and heard a deep, amused chuckle. I swallowed, my throat dry.

"Hi," Jake said after a moment.

"Hi! You have my phone."

"I do."

I smiled at the warm sound of his voice. "Where did you find it? Did I lose it on the ice? It must have fallen out of my pocket."

"Someone found it under one of the benches by the lockers and handed it into reception when I was saying goodbye and heading home."

"How did you even know it was mine?"

"Because you've dropped it in front of me twice and I recognised the dinosaur stickers."

"And they just let you let you take it?" I marvelled.

He hesitated. "Technically, no. I, uh. I didn't ask."

I cocked a hip. "Are you telling me you stole my phone?"

"I *saved* it."

"From the ice rink's lost-and-found? Couldn't you get in a lot of trouble for just walking off with someone else's property?" I was fairly sure that he could hear my smile.

"Only if you complain to management. Like I said, I didn't steal it, I saved it. I hoped you'd call yourself once you realised it was lost, and then I could get it back to you, as we're supposed to be meeting later anyway. The battery's down to five percent. I didn't think it would make it through the night."

"It wouldn't. It doesn't hold a charge for long. Hasn't been the same since I dropped it down the toilet."

He laughed. "You don't take very good care of your phone, Ben."

"There's room for improvement."

"So, now you know it's safe and you don't have to remote wipe it or anything, I can take it back to the ice rink when I go in the morning and you can drop in and get it from reception. Or…I know you're busy tonight with your surprise party, but I'd still like to take you to dinner another night. I'm on a tight schedule at the moment, but can we set something up?"

"No," I said. "I mean, yes. Yes, I'm free and I'd love to set something up, but why don't you, you know. Come over."

Did that sound like I was asking him for a booty call?

I didn't correct myself. If he wanted to interpret it that way, I was fine with it.

"You don't have to invite me to your surprise birthday party," he said. "It's cool. We just met."

I clutched Ravi's phone tighter. "I want you to come."

His voice was a touch lower when he said, "I'd like that."

"Yeah?"

"Very much." After a moment he said, "Are you going to tell me where you live?"

"Oh! Of course." I rattled off my address.

"You're only about twenty minutes away from me," he said, sounding pleased.

"Twenty minutes? Don't dawdle. I'll do my best to save you cake, but I can't make any promises."

"I won't dawdle, but I have to at least get dressed first. I just got out of the shower."

I blanked at the thought of Jake standing in his bathroom, twenty minutes away, in nothing but a towel.

Or...not even a towel.

Maybe he was air drying.

"And, Ben?" he said. "To make it clear, I'm not coming for the cake."

I laughed nervously. "Okay, so. See you soon?"

We hung up and I stood there, staring at my front door.

"He seemed delightful," Ravi said behind me, making me jump.

I whirled to face him. "He is," I said, and blushed. "He really is."

"Ooh. Look at you, going all pink."

"I am not pink."

"I was being kind. You're a weird magenta. Come on. Get in here and join the party, stuff your face, and have some bubbly before your birthday treat from the universe gets here and dicks you down for the grand finale."

"You heard the man. It's not a hookup. It's a date, not a dicking."

"Penises can still be involved."

God, I hoped so. "We were going to meet up for dinner, and there was some playful banter about a birthday kiss. That's all. He was cheering me up, because I thought I was going to have a boring and lonely birthday."

"Boring and lonely?" Ravi smacked my shoulder. "You wish. Speaking of, come on. Time to blow out the candles, cut the cake, and make a wish."

"It's too late. Mum's already cut the cake and was handing it out, last I saw. Is there even any left?"

"Doesn't matter. I got you a little wishing cake of your

own. You didn't think I was going to let you hose down the big one with all your germs and then make people *eat* it, did you? I am a *medical professional*. Only you will be eating your wishing cake."

"My...?" I tipped my head to one side and regarded him fondly. "My *wishing* cake?" That was adorable.

Ravi narrowed his eyes at me. "Don't," he warned.

"Ravi, you are the sweetest, most thoughtful friend in the whole world."

"Ugh," he said, and turned around.

He'd always been this way. He could dish it out, but he couldn't take it. I followed him. "I appreciate you. I need you to know that."

"Don't be disgusting." He sped up.

"You know what would make my birthday? Not a romantic birthday kiss after all. Just a big cuddly hug from my BFF. My bestest bud."

"Keep it up, and I'll go and tell your mother about Jake."

I sucked in a breath. "You wouldn't."

"Try me."

I did not try him.

Ravi might be the bestest BFF in the whole world and had been since I was three years old, but that didn't blind me to the fact that he could also be an absolute arsehole.

Before he noticed that I wasn't following him anymore, I changed course and whisked myself up the stairs and into the bathroom.

I didn't want fresh-from-the-shower Jake to show up and find me still wearing the jeans and hoodie I'd been wearing hours earlier on the rink. I had twenty minutes to half an hour to make this shit presentable, and I was going to make it count.

I started the shower, stripped in record time, and

hopped in even though the water hadn't even warmed up. I bravely stuck my head under the spray anyway and got down to business shampooing and soaping and scrubbing everything that needed shampooing and soaping and scrubbing.

I threw in a bit of manscaping while I was there—just the basics, I still hadn't attended the party yet—then rinsed off, hopped back out, and scrambled into clean clothes.

I slunk into the sitting room, congratulating myself on getting away with my sneaky detour, when I caught Ravi's eye from across the room and realised from the expression on his face that, no. I had not, in fact, got away with anything.

"Oh, look," he said loudly. "Our diva has finally finished his primping and has deigned to join us! Get ready to embarrass him by staring as hard as you can while he attempts to blow out all forty candles!"

"I wasn't primping," I protested. "Everyone else is dressed for the party. I'm catching up."

"Joyce!" Ravi bellowed my mother's name at top volume, aiming it at the kitchen. "Fire it up!" His expectant grin faded as we all turned and faced the same way he was facing. And waited. And waited. "Joyce?"

"I told you to give me at least three minutes warning," my mother called back. "It takes time to light this many candles. I'm going as fast as I can."

My eye twitched. "I'll go and help," I said.

Lizzie snagged the back of my jumper. "Stay right there. You can't light your own candles. I've got it."

I gazed wistfully at Lizzie as she vanished into the kitchen, and turned to see the entire room looking at me.

"Well," I said. "This is nice."

Ravi snorted.

First Dates and Birthday Cakes | 61

Thankfully, my mother appeared in the doorway a few moments later, announcing her presence with a loud, "Ta-daaa!" She held a fun-size, sugar-pink cake with a mass of blue candles crammed on it, bristling at all angles.

"Oh my god," I said and started towards her as she wobbled on her four-inch party stilettos. "Mum, don't set yourself on fire."

Ravi had lunged for her at the same time.

"For goodness' sake, boys," she said, shoving past us. "I am perfectly capable of carrying a cake."

Everyone burst into a round of applause as she set it down with a flourish on the coffee table.

She straightened, smiling. Her gaze met mine, her smile grew, and she opened her mouth.

No, I thought, digging deep and mentally projecting down the unbreakable mother-son bond forged between us on a dark and stormy night forty years ago when I entered into this troublesome life screaming at the top of my lungs, and she caught me in her loving arms. Also screaming at the top of her lungs, because I might have torn some stuff on my way out.

Don't sing.

Mum. Don't sing.

"*Happy—*" she started.

Mother, no.

"*—biiiiiirthday to yoooooou!*"

I went into a full-body clench as everyone threw themselves into it wholeheartedly, singing at me.

This morning, I woke up depressed and sure that I was at the top of the hill of life, staring down at nothing but a long dizzying slope with an open coffin at the very end.

Now, here I was, being sung at by people who loved me and liked me, or, in the case of my neighbour Brian from two doors down who was stuffing his face over by the piano, liked me well enough and wouldn't say no to free food ever.

But my god. This was painful.

I couldn't stop smiling.

Right up until I clocked that the low coffee table meant that even bending at the waist wouldn't bring my feeble lungfuls of air into close enough range to get all forty fucking candles out.

"Looks like you'll have to get on your knees for the blowing," Ravi said cheerfully. "Shouldn't be a problem for you, Ben."

I glared at him. My *parents* were right there.

Ravi grinned, unrepentant.

I was not going to get on my knees, especially now that Ravi had put that unsubtle image into everyone's head.

"Don't forget to make a wish," he said. "And remember, you have to get all the candles out in one go, or your year will be cursed. I think a demon will show up or something, I can't remember how it goes."

My mother whapped Ravi with the back of her hand.

I hyperventilated sharply, bent over, and gave it my best shot.

To my surprise, I managed to get all the candles out in one blow. I straightened, lightheaded but victorious.

"What did you wish for?" Ravi said.

At the same time, the doorbell rang.

My eyes met Ravi's across the coffee table. His glinted with mischief. Before he could make a move, I said, "I'll get it."

"Play your cards right, and you will."

"Ravi," my mother said with a suspicious note in her voice. "Did you hire a stripper again?"

"*Joyce.* I'm both shocked and offended."

I darted out of the sitting room and into the hall. If I opened the door to find a suspiciously buff cop with a boombox on the other side instead of Jake, I was going to write the whole year off, I really was.

I took a deep breath, took hold of the handle, and opened up.

5

"Hi, Ben," Jake said.

"Oh, thank god. It's you." I rushed outside and hauled the door shut behind me.

"Were you expecting someone else?"

"A stripper," I said darkly.

He smiled. "Aren't strippers more of a bachelor party kind of thing?"

"You'd think."

He'd changed from the sweatpants and hoodie he was wearing earlier into black jeans and a navy shirt under a casual jacket, with a messenger bag slung crosswise over his broad chest.

He looked amazing.

Although I had also spiffed up in the shower and changed, I wasn't fooling myself here. I probably looked as frazzled as I had when he'd first heaved me up off the ice.

Going on the unsubtle, deliberate way he checked me out, however, it seemed to be working for him. His smile deepened. "So," he said. "I brought you something."

"Really? You shouldn't have."

"I definitely should. Here." He handed me my phone.

Of course. Not a present.

Awkward.

"Thanks." I stuffed it in my back pocket. Jake raised a brow and I took it back out. "I know, I know, don't keep your phone in your back pocket." I wouldn't learn.

"I also brought you this," he said, pulling a bottle of champagne from the messenger bag. He did it with a little flourish. There was a red ribbon rosette stuck to the neck.

I took it from him. "Thank you. I haven't actually managed to have a glass of anything yet. Hey, wow. *Thank you*. This is an expensive one."

Oh, yes, very cool. Comment on the price of the gift to the gift-giver's face.

Stay classy, Ben.

Then again, I could be forgiven my momentary lapse of manners—it was a Veuve Clicquot, which cost at least fifty pounds.

He obviously hadn't just raided his fridge for a bottle of Tesco's finest sparkling French wine, left over from last Christmas and ready to regift on short notice.

"This is lovely." I clutched the cool neck of the bottle in my damp, nervous grip. "I'm really glad you came. Not because of the expensive champagne, but because it's...uh." *Because it's you*, I didn't say. He heard it anyway, going on his soft, intrigued expression. "I hope you didn't spend the afternoon thinking I ghosted you."

"No." He shifted closer. His dark-blue eyes were warm and he seemed amused. "I liberated your phone from reception before I even had a chance to make the dinner reservation."

"That's a relief."

"Mm-hmm." He reached out and brushed my hair back

from my forehead. His fingers drifted down the side of my neck and came to rest at the join between neck and shoulder. "Do you want it now?" he said, his voice low.

"You already gave it to me," I said, and waggled my phone at him..

"Your birthday kiss."

"Oh." I swayed towards him.

"Or are you going to invite me inside?"

"Oh! Yes, of course. Come on in."

He'd moved closer, crowding me against the door. I was all but in his arms as I turned to open it. His body was hot and hard behind me, and at the feel of him, of the tension strung tight between us, I couldn't repress a shiver. "On second thought," I said, turning back to face him, "now is good. I really want to kiss you and I don't know how long this party will go on."

"Bit of a rager, is it?"

"Not really. I've missed most of it and it'll probably be over in an hour. I still don't want to wait that long."

"Neither do I," he said with a smile. He placed a hand on the door beside my head and leaned in.

I attempted to grab him, but since I held his gift in one hand and my phone in the other, all I did was bang them against his hips. "Sorry," I said.

Why was I so damn nervous? I'd kissed men before, for crying out loud. Admittedly, I hadn't kissed any hot ex-figure skaters before, but this was ridiculous.

Jake tipped my chin up and lowered his head, smiling.

Before our lips met, the door clicked open behind us—because of *course* it did—and I staggered when the support at my back suddenly vanished.

Jake caught me with an arm around my waist.

"Oops," Ravi said behind me. "Thought you'd locked yourself out again. Carry on."

The door shut.

"Hold on a second," Jake told me, and rapped on the door.

"That was quick," Ravi said, opening it back up.

Jake extracted the champagne and the phone from me and shoved them at Ravi.

"Okay. I'm the butler, am I?" Ravi said. "I'll—"

Jake shut the door again. I had a second to register Ravi's laughter, then Jake pushed me flat, lifted my chin, and laid his warm mouth on mine.

It was…it was lovely.

It was a *lovely* kiss.

Sweet and soft. Confident. Not too pushy.

Not even a *little* pushy.

You'd have to be a real diva to be disappointed with a gentle, respectful birthday kiss like that, wouldn't you?

Because it was lovely.

We'd known each other a matter of hours. This was the fulfilment of a fun, jokey little promise between new acquaintances, that was all.

He hadn't returned from war. It wasn't Valentine's Day. He wasn't standing there before me after a few years of dating, a box with a ring in it burning a hole in his pocket.

Lovely.

What else was he supposed to have done, anyway?

Knocked me into the door and pinned me there with his big, hard body?

Pulled my head back with a commanding fistful of hair, opened my mouth with his and tongue-fucked me until I was limp and moaning like a hussy, scandalising Mrs

Hughes from down the road as she walked past with her elderly terrier, Dougal?

That would have been *so* inappropriate.

Jake lifted his head and smiled down at me.

"That was nice," I said. "Thank you."

His smile froze in place. A dark blond brow slowly rose. "Nice?"

I patted his chest. "It was a lovely birthday kiss. A lovely ending to the day. Lovely."

"So what I'm hearing is, it was lovely."

"Absolutely."

He made a thoughtful noise. "You didn't think something was lacking?"

Yes. "Well…"

He leaned more of his weight into me, gaze dropping to my lips.

"It's okay, though," I said. I shifted against him, and told my dick to stand down when it perked up at the light friction. "Sometimes the chemistry isn't there. No harm, no foul."

"Ben?"

"Yes?"

"Are you disappointed with your birthday kiss?"

"What kind of hard-to-please diva would—"

"Because before you go writing us off, I'd like to point out that there is a window full of people watching us—"

I gasped and whipped my head to the side. My sitting room had a bay window and yes, it was filled with faces staring out at us. I scowled and made a shooing gesture. They reluctantly dispersed.

Jake touched a hand to my jaw, redirecting my attention to him. "Other than not being keen on doing this in front of an audience, I'm hoping to come in and hang out with you for a while, and I'm trying to get my boner to go down first. Kissing you the way I want to kiss you is *not* going to help me achieve that goal."

He had a boner? I arched my hips to suss out the pants situation, and he sucked in a sharp breath.

He caught me and held me still. "I'd hate for you to go on thinking that the chemistry isn't there. Because I think it is." He ducked down and murmured against my mouth, "Let me show you."

He kissed me again.

This one was also quick, but it wasn't soft and it wasn't gentle.

It was demanding, and hot, and before he pulled away, a teasing, there-and-gone flicker of tongue shot a bolt of arousal through my stomach and down my thighs. My fingers flexed into his sides.

"What do you think?" he said. "Better?"

I stared up at him. He held my jaw and rubbed a thumb over my damp bottom lip, eyes intense. "A little," I said.

"A little?" He seemed legitimately annoyed this time.

I shrugged. "There's potential."

Jake narrowed his eyes at me. "Potential."

"Yeah." Hiding my giddy smile, I turned in his arms and opened the door. The noise of the music and people talking loudly washed over us.

Jake kept his arm around my waist, and as we crossed the threshold, he tugged me backwards into him and kissed the side of my neck, nipping lightly. "You'd better believe there's *potential*," he growled in my ear before he let me go.

I believed it. In fact, there was such an overabundance of potential, I was having a hard time not saying screw the party, and running him up the stairs and into my bedroom right now.

"Let's get you a glass of champagne," I said instead, leading him to the kitchen.

I found the Veuve Clicquot sitting in the fridge—I made a mental note to thank Ravi for his excellent butlering—and brought it out.

"Why don't you save it for another time?" Jake said. "It would be a shame to open it if it hasn't been chilled properly."

"What kind of host do you think I am? I'm not saving the good stuff for myself—"

"You don't have to save it for yourself. I'd be happy to help you drink it. Later. Or on another occasion, even."

We locked eyes as he took the bottle out of my slack hand before I dropped it.

"Unless I'm assuming too much here?" he said quietly, setting the bottle on the counter.

"I don't know. Maybe you are. I'll need some more detail on what, exactly, you're assuming before I can give you a clear answer on that."

"Detail," he said. "All right." He nudged me against the counter and put a hand either side of me. The handle of the cutlery drawer was jammed into my arse, but I didn't mention it. The sensation of his body on mine was too delicious to give up. "Here's what I'm assuming. I'm assuming that later, when the party has broken up and everyone has gone, you'll ask me to stay just a little longer. How am I doing so far?"

"That sounds very possible."

"I'll stay, and I'll help you tidy up the mess."

"That sounds very helpful."

First Dates and Birthday Cakes | 71

"I'm a helpful guy."

Helpful. Generous. Sexy as hell.

He continued, "Once we've done that, I was thinking that I'd tease you until you broke down and begged me to kiss you."

"That sounds very intriguing. Although I don't think I'll need all that much teasing. Or any. I think you're teasing me enough right now, in fact. So we can skip that part and go straight to the kissing. As in, the moment the last plate hits the dishwasher, get your lips on me."

"Good to know," he said. "But I think I'd like to make you desperate first."

He was going to have a problem if he wanted to *make* me desperate.

I already *was* desperate.

I rewrote our little script in my head: instead of begging him to kiss me, I'd just jump him.

"What else are you assuming?" I asked. "Anything after the kissing?"

"I'm assuming that it will be time for bed by then."

My hands had somehow wandered to his waist, and they tightened at the thought of Jake sprawled out on my bed.

"At which point," he said with a big grin, "I'll wish you goodnight and head on home."

I sighed. "That sounds amaz—wait, you're going to what?"

"Head home."

"Not, I don't know. Drag me upstairs, and throw me on my bed and have your filthy way with me? Because you could assume that. If you want."

"No."

"Oh. Well. That sounds...lovely."

"You seem disappointed again, Ben."

"What? No, no. Not at all." I eased out from between him and the counter. "I'm going to get that glass of champagne for you. And a piece of cake."

I had clearly let myself get carried away, because I'd been assuming a whole other scenario.

Which was stupid.

I met him a few hours ago. We'd planned on having a date, a birthday kiss, and that was all. There had been no mention of sex at any point. Or anything else, come to that.

The cupboard where I kept the glasses was empty. The sink was full of them. I turned the hot tap on and snagged the detergent.

"And then," Jake continued, "*assuming* you don't lose your phone between now and tomorrow morning—a bold assumption, perhaps, but I'm going with it—I *assumed* that I'd call you, and see if I could talk you into going out on that first date I had planned. Which will now technically be a second date."

I turned to find him watching me with amusement. And heat. A lot of heat.

"Oh."

"I don't want to fuck and run here, Ben," he said. "If that's all you want, then let me know. We can do that. But..." He rubbed a hand up the back of his neck and glanced at the ground before looking back up at me. "I kind of really want to date you."

"I kind of really want to date you, too," I said breathily. For god's sake. I was forty. There were teenagers out there with more game than me.

"Yeah?" he said.

"Yes."

We stared at each other.

"Although," I said, watching his pupils expand, "I still vote that you drag me upstairs and—"

He laughed. "I'd love to, trust me. I can't. It might be a Sunday tomorrow, but I have to be at the rink by eight a.m., which means getting up even earlier. I'm too old to be crawling home at two in the morning for a few hours sleep."

"Too old?" I scoffed. "You're in your thirties. You're a baby. Back when I was your age, I could party all night and *kill* it at work the next day. Besides, impress me enough and I'll let you spend the night."

Wow. While I was at it, why didn't I just fall to my knees right there and beg the man?

"Back when you were my age? You mean three whole years ago, you were regularly out partying until dawn?"

"Yes. That's exactly the sort of thing I was doing. I'm a very glamorous and exciting man. I'm sure you'll agree, once you get to know me."

I hadn't partied until dawn for—nope. I wasn't going to ruin the moment by working out that particular number.

Jake was standing close and smiling down at my nonsense when someone cleared their throat behind him. We both jumped.

It was my mother.

"Hello," she said brightly, crossing the kitchen with her hand outstretched. "I'm Joyce, Ben's mum. It's very nice to meet you…?"

"Jakub," he said, taking her hand for a polite shake. "Good to meet you, Joyce."

Instead of concluding the social ritual like a normal person would and letting the man go, my mother expertly turned her grip, her Tiffany bracelet loaded with charms jangling, and strode off, hauling him after her.

"Jake," she said, "there is a piece of cake in the other

room with your name on it. We're down to the last couple of slices, but don't worry, I've got Barry standing guard. Barry's his father, in case you didn't know. Did you know?"

"I did not."

"Interesting. Either he's ashamed of us, or this is new. Is this new?"

"It is." Jake shot a laughing glance over at me as he permitted my tiny mother in her ridiculous shoes to march him out of the kitchen.

"You're not subtle, Mother," I called after her.

The woman thought she had Columbo-level interrogation skills. She thought she was Sherlock Holmes, Miss Marple, and Benoit Blanc, all wrapped up in a five-foot-nothing package. Nobody could convince her she was about as subtle as a sledgehammer.

"If you told me anything at all about your life," she said sweetly, "I wouldn't have to try to be."

I told her plenty.

"Now," she said, "Barry might be standing guard and I do love that man, but he's a complete pushover. If he fails in his mission and we don't get you a piece of the good cake, I'm afraid you'll have to settle for some of Ben's wishing cake."

"Do not feed him any of my wishing cake," I said. "It's unsanitary."

"It's not ideal," Mum conceded, "but hopefully Jakub won't mind, since the two of you are dating." She tipped her head all the way back to look up into Jake's face. "Are you dating?"

"Yes," he said firmly. "We're dating."

I chased after them, despite wanting to take the coward's way out and stay in the kitchen to throw back a couple of glasses of champagne—or a bottle—for courage. I lost them three steps into the sitting room, getting waylaid by Lizzie, who wanted to know if I'd stopped having a crisis now that the universe had seen fit to drop a cake, a party, and a hot guy on me all in one day.

She also wanted to know how, exactly, I'd managed to swing it. Vision board, affirmations, witchcraft? She was turning thirty soon and would like a few tips.

I told her to screw the toxic positivity and marry Ravi because we all knew it was inevitable, and by the time I'd extracted myself, it was too late to save Jake. My mother had whisked him into the thick of the party, and, no doubt, cranked up the interrogation as my triumphant father handed over a laden plate.

Knowing Mum, she was grilling him about his job, any past relationships, where he saw this going, what were his thoughts on kids and/or dogs, was he busy at Christmas and all sorts of horrifyingly nosy things, unaware that when Jake said it was new, he meant today.

It was new *today*.

Jake appeared to take it all in stride and I marvelled at his cool. What must life be like, I wondered, if you were relaxed enough to be able to just roll with things.

Perhaps if I spent more time with him, some of his cool would rub off on me.

I glazed over at the thought of Jake rubbing off on me, and flinched when Ravi cheerfully said, "Stop eye-fucking him, mate, we all know what's up. Quite the show you put on out there."

"Quite the show?" I said indignantly. "It was a little kiss. There wasn't even any tongue." There had been a little bit of tongue.

"So much sexual tension, the street lights were flickering," Ravi said, coming to stand next to me where I was leaning against the wall, staring at Jake. He shoved a piece of wishing cake at me.

"Thank you," I said. "And the street lights aren't even on." I made short work of the cake and chased the final smudges of buttercream on the plate with a forefinger. I stuck the finger in my mouth and made sure I got it all.

Looking up, I made inadvertent eye contact with Jake across the room. I noticed with interest that his composure wasn't *quite* as unshakeable as it seemed at first glance. His cheekbones were dusted with colour and his lips parted as he watched me.

I pulled my finger out slowly, and almost died when I realised my bemused father, talking to Jake, was also watching.

"Shit." I hunched in on myself, yanking Ravi in front of me as a shield.

"It's a good thing you're going to get you some," Ravi said, obligingly shifting his tall frame between us. He was my shield and my knight, the noblest of men. "I've never seen you this wound up before."

"I'm not getting it tonight," I said glumly.

"Why not?" Ravi sounded outraged.

"He wants to date me first."

"What a tosser."

I pressed my forehead between his shoulder blades and groaned. "I really like him, Ravi."

Ravi turned to face me. "I know you do, Ben. Everyone in this room knows you do."

"What if...?"

"What if what?"

"What if he's...you know." I hesitated, hardly believing I was even saying it. "What if he's the one?"

Ravi snorted. "You've known the guy for ten minutes.

First Dates and Birthday Cakes | 77

Why don't you wait until you've taken him out for a test drive before you start fretting about the rest of your life together? He might be a damp squib, you never know."

There I was, once again cracking open my quivering and hopeful heart, showing my vulnerability, reaching out for reassurance from my oldest friend. And there Ravi was, being crass. "Take him for a *test drive*?"

"Yeah. Jump in the driver's seat. Stick your key in his ignition. Open up that throttle. Burn some rubber." He held out his hands. "A test drive."

I stared at him. "Do you have any romance in you? At all?"

"Yes, but unlike you, I try not to let it drown out simple reason." He sighed dramatically. "Ben. You're an idiot. What if he *is* the one? Why are you even asking me that? Happily ever after. That's what if."

I'd never really seen myself having a happily ever after. Not really.

Then again, I'd never really seen myself turning forty either. It wasn't that I'd expected to die young, but forty was one of those things that had always seemed distant, nebulous, belonging to the future.

Like it or not, the future was now. It had caught up. I was forty. Maybe I could have a happily ever after, too?

"Stop taking it all *so* seriously," Ravi said, "and eat more cake."

"I can't help it. I'm a worrier."

"Yeah. I know. And I love you, you weirdo."

I looked up into his warm brown eyes. "I love you."

"Happy birthday, mate." He hooked an arm around my neck, leaned down and pressed a smacking kiss square on my lips.

I was still squawking about it when he turned and

bellowed, "What do you say, party people? One more rendition of Ben's favourite song before we wrap it up?" He launched right in. "*Haaaaaaappy biiiiiirthday...*"

I tried to bolt, but Ravi caught me and held me against the wall while I endured, feeling like the luckiest man in the world, and the party wrapped up.

6

When he'd said he wanted to date me before he did anything else to me, Jake wasn't kidding. If you counted my birthday party as our first date, then tonight we were on our fourth.

I was definitely being romanced.

Our second date had been back at the rink. As a skating coach, Jake's hours were more flexible than my office-bound nine to five. He often worked on weekday evenings, meaning that while I was finishing up and leaving the office for the day, he'd be coming off a free afternoon and be heading into evening coaching sessions.

We managed to find an overlapping couple of hours early in the week to meet in the small cafe overlooking the ice. We had coffee (mine was decaf), talking and laughing and sitting unnecessarily close to each other until his class showed up. I hung out for another half an hour after that to watch him at work, admiring his patience and unflagging good humour with his young hopefuls.

When I went over to the barrier to say goodbye, he spotted me at once and zipped over with the arousing, competent grace that had captivated me from the first moment I saw him.

He thudded gently into the boards and gripped the edge to lean over and catch my lips, all in one smooth move. He kept it to a quick peck, so as not to scandalise his students—who whooped and clapped—and I walked out smiling like a fool.

If I hadn't already known that my heart was in big trouble as far as Jake was concerned, that kiss would have done it.

On our third date, we grabbed a quick sandwich for lunch, eating on the go as we strolled around a small park midway between the rink and my office. I lingered as long as I could, reluctant to leave, and ended up speed-walking back to my car, but not before Jake had caught me by the shirtfront, reeled me in, and given me a kiss that made it impossible to concentrate on work for the rest of the afternoon.

We'd texted, although not much. Flirting via text wasn't my strong suit. It really wasn't Jake's strong suit.

His thirst-trap selfie game was on point, though, I'll give him that.

The number of locker room and gym mirror shots I now had stored in my camera roll would have given teenage Ben carpal tunnel syndrome.

Forty-something Ben was smart enough to pace himself after the first twinge.

And here we were, two weeks later, finally on a proper date, with no one having to end it and hurry off to work.

Jake had picked me up from my house and driven us into Oxford, and I was impressed. The restaurant was fancy as hell. It served amazing Polish food that sorely tested my self-control, it was the classiest, most romantic dining establishment I'd ever been in, and I couldn't wait to get out of there.

"Dessert, gentlemen?" the waiter asked as he was clearing the plates from our main course. He leaned past me, arm brushing my shoulder, and turned his head to give me a challenging look.

I opened my mouth to decline, but Jake beat me to it.

"Yes, please." He reached across the table to place a warm hand over mine. I'd been twisting the stem of my wineglass between restless fingers, turning the glass one way then the other, making it glint in the candlelight. "I told you I was going to spoil you, Ben," he said. "That means you get everything you want tonight. Everything." He backed that last, firm, word up with a serious smoulder that had my cheeks heating.

I could hardly blame him for thinking that dessert was at the top of my list. He had, after all, watched me scoff my wishing cake on our first date, two muffins on our second date, and a Danish pastry the size of my face on our third date.

What I really wanted, though, was to scoot him out of the restaurant and into the car, and get us back home, where I could have him all to myself.

I didn't even care what happened once I had him there.

I didn't care if we had the wild and passionate sex that had been brewing from the moment we met, canoodled like teenagers on my sofa, or hung out and talked into the night.

I just wanted to be with him.

"Of course," the waiter said. "I'll bring you the menu."

He whisked our plates away with admirable efficiency and returned with the dessert menus. He thrust one out in Jake's direction, earning himself a narrow look, and sashayed over to my side of the table to hand me mine. "Thank you," I said, reaching for it.

Instead of passing it to me, he set it on the table, rested one hand next to it and the other on the back of my chair, and leaned in. He ran a slender forefinger down the list and stopped, giving it a little tap. "For you, I recommend the tiramisu," he said, turning his head to look me in the eye from three whole inches away. "Italian, but still delicious. Melts on the tongue." His eyes flicked down and back up. "Will give you a rush, I guarantee."

"Oh?" I said with interest, tugging the menu out from under his finger and scanning it. I glanced up at Jake. "I usually go for the brownie, but I'm up for trying something new. What do you think?"

Jake was sprawled back in his chair, watching. "Yeah," he said. "Sounds good. We'll have that. Let's share." He cut his gaze to the waiter. "Two spoons."

The waiter straightened and sent him a flirty smile. "Of course."

Jake watched him shake his perky little arse all the way across the restaurant, swinging between the crowded tables with practiced ease. Before he disappeared through the door to the kitchen, the waiter cast a quick look over his shoulder.

That flirty smile widened.

"Wow," Jake said.

"Uh." I was startled at him brazenly checking the guy out right in front of me. "You...? You think he's hot?"

"What?" Jake said. Now he seemed startled. "Paweł? No."

"You know him?"

"Yes. This is his grandmother's restaurant, and he used to go out with my cousin."

"But you never...?"

"No. God, no. He's an okay guy, but he's not exactly my type. Too young, too full of himself, and far too bossy. That aside, he seems more into you."

"*Me*?

"Ben, he's been flirting with you since he seated us."

"No. Has he?"

Jake's eyebrows lifted. "He practically had you in his arms a second ago."

He had? I thought I'd remember that.

"Seriously," Jake said. "The bit with the menu? Leaning all over you, telling you what to order?"

"It was a recommendation. I thought it was nice of him."

"Are you joking?"

"It was nice!"

"And you didn't notice that he was close enough to kiss you while he was being nice?"

"No?"

"How could you not notice?"

I smiled at him. "Why would I, when I've got you sitting right in front of me?"

Jake's tense expression smoothed out and he stared at me. "Do you actually want dessert?" he said suddenly.

"Not really. I'm stuffed."

"All right." Jake stood up. "Back in a minute," he said, and strode off.

When he returned, he was smiling. He was also carrying our coats. "That's that sorted," he said. "Let's go."

"What?"

"Yep. Come on, let's go. Up you get."

He had me out of my chair and was herding me out of the restaurant before I knew what was happening. "What about the tiramisu?" I said.

"I cancelled it."

I turned, bumping into him, and tried to walk back into the restaurant. "What about the bill?"

"For goodness' sake. Ben, I paid it."

"What's the hurry all of a sudden?"

"You want to know what the hurry is?" He gripped my shoulders and pointed me in the direction of the car. "The hurry is, I've watched Paweł flirt with you all night and you apparently didn't notice." He nudged me ahead of him. "On the one hand, that's good. I didn't want you to notice him. On the other hand, it's bad. If you didn't pick up on Paweł's interest, then there's a good chance that you have no idea quite how into you I am. So I decided to be a bit more direct. As in, get you into bed and get inside you direct. Hard to misunderstand that level of interest."

My knees weakened at the heavy meaning in his eyes. "I like direct. Direct is good."

"Excellent. In the car."

He hustled me into the car, we had a tense drive home, and then we were in my house.

As soon as the front door clicked shut, Jake was on me.

He hooked an arm around my waist and dragged me in and up against his hard body, ducking his head and getting his mouth on mine.

I threw my arms around his shoulders to keep my balance as he walked me backwards through the hall and into the sitting room, still kissing me.

I stopped him and drew back, trying to catch my breath. "We're going the wrong way," I said.

"Hmm? We're what?" He drew my bottom lip into his mouth and sucked gently.

"Oh, *god*."

He smiled against me and did something with his tongue that sent a rush of sensation from my scalp to the soles of my feet. Cupping my jaw with both hands, he held me firmly as he did it again, then again, and again. My hips started a slow, involuntary rock into his.

I caught his wrists and gasped into his mouth, "Bedroom! Bedroom's up the stairs."

"Right." He pulled away and stared down at me. His eyes were wide and dark, cheeks flushed, lips damp and swollen. He swallowed hard.

"I mean..." I trailed off, getting distracted as I gripped his lovely butt and squeezed. "Uh. It's not as if there's a law saying we *have* to do it in a bed."

Then again, I didn't really want to have sex on my sitting room floor.

Getting overcome with passion and grinding around on a carpet wasn't as much fun as it might sound, especially when you're the one on the bottom being rhythmically and enthusiastically shoved back and forth over fibres not designed to be kind to delicate areas.

Jake's hands were restless on my sides. He curved them around my ribs and tugged me into him, kissing my neck and adding a hair-raising scrape of teeth.

I moaned in delight. Then, "Wait!"

He stopped and pressed his forehead into my shoulder—having to hunch down to do it—panting quietly. "You okay?"

"Yes," I said. "*Yes*, I am spectacular. This is great. More of this."

He lifted my chin and went for my mouth again.

I hummed into the kiss, making a noise of complaint when he stopped it. "What...?" I said, chasing after him.

"You wanted to wait."

"No. Well, just for a moment. I wanted to say let's go upstairs. I want you in a bed."

He shifted, putting a hand between us to adjust himself. My stomach muscles jumped at the graze of his knuckles against my dick. "Don't know if I can walk," he said. "You've got me so hard I might hurt myself."

"I can fix that." Keeping my eyes on his, I leaned back and popped the button of his dark indigo date jeans. I slowly dragged the tab of his zipper down an inch.

His breath hitched and his hips bumped into mine.

"How's that?" I said. "Do you think you can walk now?"

His lids lowered. "No."

"Need a bit more room?"

"Yeah."

I unzipped another inch and slid my hand into his jeans. I measured the length of his erection with my palm and my gaze bounced up to his, eyes wide.

He grinned.

No wonder he had concerns about walking without doing damage. There was a lot crammed in here. I pushed the heel of my palm against him teasingly and he groaned, flexing into me.

"*Ben.*"

I unzipped him the rest of the way and spread the fly wide open, admiring the view. "Can you walk now?"

"Mhm. Maybe."

Only one way to find out. I squirmed out of his arms and strode for the door, looking over my shoulder.

He came after me.

I sped up, and put some attitude into it.

Fine, I strutted.

He caught me at the bottom of the stairs, turned me in his arms for a deep, fierce kiss, then turned me back around and shoved me ahead of him.

We made it up the stairs and stumbled into the bedroom

wrapped around each other. Jake backed me towards the bed, and as soon as my legs hit the mattress, he pushed me down.

He kneed my legs apart and loomed over me, taking a long, simmering look.

I stretched out, doing my best to look seductively inviting, then ruined it by scrambling backwards and rolling off the other side of the bed.

Before he even had a chance to question what I was doing, I'd whisked the curtains shut, snapped the bedside lamp on, and thrown myself back onto the mattress. A pillow bounced and toppled to the floor.

I stretched out again, this time in the middle of the bed.

Jake smiled. "You can move pretty fast for a forty-year-old," he said.

I reached behind me, snagged another pillow, and hurled it at him.

He caught it and tossed it back. His smiled drained away. "Ben?" he said, his voice rough.

"Yeah?" My voice, in contrast, was ridiculously breathy.

"Get naked for me."

No problem.

I unbuttoned my cuffs and moved on to the rest of the buttons down the front of my shirt, pausing when Jake tutted.

"Slower," he said. "I want to savour this moment."

My cheeks heated but I did as he said and slowed down, hoping that he couldn't see the fine tremble in my hands. "Why don't you get over here and show me exactly how you like it," I suggested.

Instead of replying, he wrapped his big hands around my knees and gave me a firm tug down the bed. The duvet bunched beneath me as he dragged me right to the edge and arranged my legs either side of his. I expected him to help out with the buttons but he just stared down at me, still gripping my knees.

I stared back for a frozen moment, then got to work. When I tried to sit up, he shook his head and pressed me flat. He watched intently, his gaze moving between my face and my busy fingers.

I didn't know quite what wonders he expected to be unveiled here, but I really hoped that he was in a froth of impatience to encounter a plain white t-shirt and a fairly average man-chest, because that's all I was packing.

He set a hand at the side of my neck and feathered his fingers gently up and down, drifting between my collarbone and my jaw. I was wound so tight with anticipation that my whole body jerked at his touch and I stalled.

"Keep going," he said roughly.

I made quick work of the rest of the buttons and dropped my hands to my sides, fisting the rumpled duvet.

Jake stroked the panels of my shirt aside. He ran a palm over my chest, dragging it down my stomach to my waistband. He traced his fingers along the edge, before sliding his hand up and under the hem of my t-shirt.

The moment he hit bare skin, I moaned and my body curled in on itself. Just from that light touch.

He flattened his hand and pushed upward firmly, shoving the t-shirt up to my armpits. He stopped, leaving it there. I flexed helplessly beneath his focused attention.

"Trousers, now," he said.

I didn't waste any time popping the button and unzipping the fly. I braced my toes on the floor and arched my hips up, squirming my trousers and boxers down as far as they would go with Jake still standing between my thighs.

He took over, grabbing hold of the loose fabric and

hauling it the rest of the way. At least, he tried—he could only get so far before he was thwarted by the shoes we'd both forgotten I was still wearing.

With a strained huff of laughter, he dropped to a crouch and removed my shoes one at a time. He set them onto the bedroom floor beside him and completed my de-trousering, setting trousers and boxers on top of my shoes in a haphazard pile.

I leaned up on my elbows and gazed down the length of my half-naked body, my eyes widening as I absorbed the sight of him right there, pinning my legs open with his broad shoulders, face a scant few inches from my excited dick.

My breathing picked up, loud and obvious.

He smiled but he didn't look all that amused. It was far too dark and fierce for amusement. He leaned forwards and dropped a teasing kiss to the tip of my dick.

"*Oh*," I said, and my hips bucked up.

Flattening a hand on my stomach and pressing me down, he straightened. "Shirt and t-shirt," he said.

"Right." I scrambled up to sitting and yanked it all off.

My clothes comprehensively disposed of, he pushed closer between my legs and reached down to cup my face. He rubbed his thumbs gently over my cheekbones as I held his wrists.

Slowly, he bent down, bringing our mouths together, and he kissed me.

It started off light.

It escalated quickly.

Within seconds, he'd wrangled me up the mattress towards the pillows and had stretched out over me. I had his shirt untucked and bunched up to his arms, he'd kicked his shoes off, and my hands were stuffed down the back of his jeans, holding a double handful of firm butt cheeks in tight, silky black boxer briefs.

"Ben," he said, breaking away. His hips pushed into mine when I squeezed my insane handful, hard. "Ben, let me get my jeans off."

"Yes," I said, and yanked at his boxers. "And these." I wanted his bare skin beneath my hands.

"Yeah." He laughed roughly. "You have to let go," he said. "Just for a minute."

"Sorry, but I don't know if I can."

He rose up to his knees above me, reached behind him, and grasped my wrists. He gave a gentle pull.

"Nope," I said, digging my fingers in. "It's impossible. Can't do it. Feels too good."

He stripped his shirt off, his undershirt followed, and he moved to straddle me with his jeans at mid-thigh and his spectacular bubble butt in my hands. The front of his boxer briefs was damp.

I licked my lips.

"Ben," he said hoarsely.

"Look, I can't help it if this is the most amazing arse I've ever felt in my life. Why is it so amazing, anyway?" I kneaded the firm flesh, testing its smooth resilience. "How many hours of squats per day does this take?"

"Not squats. Skating. It's the best workout in the world for glutes. And thighs." He moved over me restlessly. "Why don't you check out my thighs?"

Great idea.

I slid my hands down to the backs of his legs, and around to palm his quads. They were hard and tense beneath my questing touch. It was tough to really appreciate it, though, as Jake seized the opportunity to push his boxer briefs down, freeing his cock.

I clutched his thighs, fingers spasming, then urgently tugged him closer.

"Hang on," he said, working his briefs down. After a short flurry of movement that included leaving me bereft for a moment, he managed to get them and his jeans all the way off, and get back on me.

I sighed with relief at the feel of his big, naked body.

"Yeah," he said, getting comfortable, notching his hips between my thighs, his pelvis snug to mine. "Better."

I went back to holding his arse as soon as it was in reach, stroking it, revelling in the dense, taut muscle under hot, silky skin.

He framed my head with his forearms and ducked down for a kiss. I opened to him eagerly. We kissed as if the world was ending, or so it felt. I couldn't stop touching him, running my hands down his back, holding his ribs, his thighs, his arse.

He flexed into me, sliding our cocks together, controlling the kiss. I hadn't exactly been chill about any of this in the first place, but within minutes I was a writhing, panting mess beneath him.

Then he stroked my whole body with his in the sort of body roll that I'd only ever seen the confident, hot boys do on a club dance floor, and I almost lost it.

"Ahhhh," I said, my head digging back into the pillow and my spine arching.

He backed off, gasping out, "What do you want, Ben? Do you want to keep going like this, or—"

"More," I said. "I want more."

I wanted everything.

"Yes," he said. "Yes, stay right there and I'll go and get—"

"Don't you dare go anywhere. Here." I shoved a hand under the pillow I was half-lying on and dug around. I'd stashed a condom and lubricant there before leaving, with the intention of coming across as all cool and suave when the time came.

Unfortunately, my stash must have been under the other pillow, the one I'd knocked to the floor earlier, and even though I swept my hand over the mattress where it should be, I came up empty. "Shit," I said. "Hang on a minute."

I squirmed about beneath him until he got the message and helpfully lifted up. Not far, though.

I turned onto my front, elbowed my way up to the top of the bed, and peered around. Had it fallen...? I lunged across the mattress to look over the side of the bed, then under it. Nope.

Perhaps it had got wedged between the mattress and the headboard? I pushed onto my knees and elbows and wriggled a hand into the narrow gap. My fingers closed around the packet and the lubricant. "Aha!" I said in triumph.

"Got it?" Jake said.

"Yes, I—oh."

He dragged me backwards and lay down on top of me again. I turned my head to the side, moaning when he kissed the back of my neck and scraped his teeth over the top of my spine.

I arched up, pushing my arse into his pelvis. His cock was hot and hard against me, and he rolled his hips in response. His arms were tucked close into my sides.

He was *shaking*.

I twisted an arm up and behind me, cupping his neck and drawing him down to kiss me. The angle was awkward and it was messy, but our mouths brushed tenderly together.

"God, Ben," he said. "You feel so good." He pushed a hand between us and gripped my arse.

"Yes," I said. "Yeah, like this."

"Yeah? On your belly?"

"Mm." I arched against him again.

"Okay. Okay." He kissed me then lifted away and eased the condom and tube of lubricant out of my tight fingers. Foil crinkled quietly, followed by the soft click of the lubricant.

I sucked in a breath when he touched me, going straight between my cheeks. "Hurry," I said, shuffling my thighs apart as best I could while being pinned beneath him.

His fingers were knowing and firm, and he didn't waste time. "You tell me if it hurts, or—"

"Of course, yes. I will. I'm good. I won't need much."

"No?" he said with interest, slowing down the stroke of the finger he had inside me already. He added another and I hummed in pleasure.

"No, I...may have been, uh. Working up to it. To this. You. For a while, I—*uhn.*" I choked. "Yes! *There*! Right there!"

He laughed and repeated the slow drag inside me. "Right here?"

"No! Left a bit! Left a bit!"

"Uh-huh." He adjusted, and his next lazy stroke hit the spot unerringly with a firm rub, telling me that he'd been avoiding it on purpose.

I growled and pushed up to my elbows.

He pushed me back down with a heavy hand between my shoulder blades. "Tell me more about this 'working up to it' business. It sounds interesting. Sounds like the sort of thing I'd like to hear about."

My thighs widened reflexively and I pushed into my knees, rippling up into his strokes. The hand between my shoulders slid down to play at the small of my back. The weight of it made me want to push up more, to arch even more. I didn't fight the urge, and Jake's breath caught at my shameless display.

I buried my face in the duvet, working my arse up and down into his hands, and said, "I may have embarked upon a stretching routine. Possibly involving some toys. *Possibly*."

I was being coy. It definitely involved some toys.

I had quite the selection, since toys and my imagination had constituted the bulk of my sex life for the last few years.

"You certainly seem...flexible." His voice roughened as he added another finger.

"Oh, I am," I said. Moaned, practically. Wow. Listen to me and my sultry voice. "Where it counts, anyway."

My face burned. I couldn't believe I was boasting about the flexibility of my butthole.

He leaned down and said in my ear, "Have you been preparing yourself for me, Ben? Is that what you're trying to say?"

"Yes." I pushed up demandingly.

"All right, then." He settled over me, taking his time getting comfortable, arranging himself.

"*Jake*."

He adjusted his hard cock, wedging it between my cheeks and gliding between them for a few long, sweet strokes. I fisted the duvet, moving with him.

His breath shattered over the back of my neck. He adjusted again and guided himself achingly slowly inside. I made an impatient noise and tried to shove back but he had me at his mercy and refused to be hurried. It went on and on until, finally, he bottomed out.

We both held still, shaking. When Jake's hands came over mine, I spread my fingers wide. He slotted his between them, as if we'd done this a thousand times already.

First Dates and Birthday Cakes | 95

I said his name again. This time it was a beseeching whisper.

"Yeah." He drew his hips back and surged forwards. I felt the slide of him, deep inside.

He did it again, then again, then again.

The room filled with our gasps and moans—mostly mine—and the sound of Jake's hips smacking against my arse as he ramped up the intensity of his thrusts. He had some serious power in those skating-sculpted thighs of his. It felt like I was being spanked. He pushed up onto his forearms and sped up, then lifted up and away.

Air rushed cold over my back without his body laid over mine, and I was about to complain when his big hands closed around my hips and he hauled me back onto his cock, draping me over his lap with my thighs as wide as they'd go.

This was a new position for me and, I thought, very possibly a new favourite.

I heaved up onto an elbow, twisting around to get a look at him. It was awkward—my neck wasn't as flexible as other body parts, sadly—but I saw enough.

He was sitting back on his heels, staring down at me, moving his hips with tight, sinuous rolls that did incredible things to the flexing muscles in his hard abdomen.

His face was flushed, his dark-blue eyes were narrowed and intense, and his gaze flicked up to lock with mine. Having caught me watching, he put a bit of swagger into the next few thrusts and I choked.

Jake's lips curled up at one side. "You like that?" he said.

"Do it again," I said. "Harder."

He tightened his fingers around my hips, thrust hard, and at the same time he dragged me onto him, bouncing me on his dick.

"Oh my *god*," I said, and whimpered into the duvet.

After that, things devolved into a fast and frantic tempo. My ears were ringing and my vision—when I managed to blink my eyes open—wavered at the relentless pace.

Jake. Just. Didn't. Stop.

It got to the point where my gasps and moans were stitched together into an almost continuous wail when he suddenly pulled out and flipped me over.

Stunned, I lay there on my back, panting up at him, eyes stinging with salt. He collapsed on top of me, holding my jaw as he kissed me.

"Ben," he said. "This is…I want you so much. I just…holy shit, I want you so much."

I curled my arms around him and held him tight. "Me too," I said when he gave me the chance to speak between harsh, biting kisses. "Me too."

He hitched his hips up, reached between us, and guided himself back inside. "Can I…? Is it okay like this? I want—"

I hissed with pleasure at the feel of him, hooking a leg around his thigh and doing my best to pull him closer.

"—I want to see you," he was saying. "Want to watch you." He leaned back, eyes intent on my face as he thrust into me and held himself deep, grinding his hips in tiny circles.

My neck arched and I gasped up at the ceiling.

"Can I?" he said, his voice rough. "Can I have you like this?"

"Yeah. Yes."

He groaned and ducked his head to catch my mouth with his, licking deep, owning me completely.

I brought my other leg up, gripping his sides with my thighs, and goaded him on.

It didn't take long after that. A few more rapid thrusts, and he was shaking hard against me.

I held him, cupping his buttocks and encouraging him, pulling him rhythmically into me as he came. He slowed his frantic pace to a gentle glide, his harsh pants softening.

My breathing didn't soften at all. I was still gasping desperately.

Jake unhooked my legs and got a hand on my dick while he was still inside me. He gazed down into my face as he stroked me, working me fast and hard. I wailed, body seizing up as the climax that had been crashing around in my pelvis drew down tight and detonated.

When I blinked the sweat out of my eyes, Jake had pulled me into his arms and turned us onto our sides. At some point while I was still reeling, he'd withdrawn from my body and dealt with the condom. I felt him now, spent and soft against me. He stroked a warm hand up and down my waist, drifting down to my thigh and back up to my ribs. Up and down. Up and down.

I blinked at him, completely without words.

I'd suspected that having sex with Jake would be something special, and yet I still felt blindsided by it.

He smiled and drew my leg up and over his hip, tucking us as close together as it was possible to get.

He leaned in and kissed me.

It was sweet, so sweet, and soft. He whispered my name. I clutched him tight and he whispered it again.

It sounded like a promise.

7

Three years later...
"I don't know," I said to Ravi. "I'm not really a fan of surprise parties."

We were sitting in a pub in Oxford, not far from the hospital where Ravi worked. It was the sort of place that tourists enjoyed for its black-beamed ceilings, its quirky little rooms and eight-hundred-year history, and locals enjoyed for its quiet, back-lane location and decent prices.

Close to ten p.m. on a Thursday night, the pub was hot, loud, and packed.

We'd managed to snag the last two available barstools, and if the guy shoved up behind me pressed any closer, he'd scoot me clean off my stool and onto Ravi's lap.

I shot him a stern glare over my shoulder. He eased back with an unconcerned shrug.

Earlier that morning, Ravi had left me an unsettling voicemail, instructing me to meet him there after work because he had a *fantastic* idea that I was going to *love*.

Needless to say, I'd been worrying about his fantastic idea all day. And I was right to do so.

I'd heard it.

I didn't love it.

Ravi set his pint of Guinness on the polished wood of the bar between us. "What do you mean, you're not a fan?" he demanded. "You loved your surprise fortieth, Ben. It was the best day of your life."

"It was a good day," I said. "In the end. I wouldn't go so far as to say it was the best, though."

"Name one day that was better. *One.* I'll wait."

I just looked at him.

"Ugh." Ravi pulled a face. "You're going to say the day Jake moved in and you degenerates had a sex marathon and shagged in every room, aren't you?"

"Yes." Hell, yes.

It was the athletic achievement of my life.

I'd never orgasmed that many times in a single weekend. I hadn't known I could.

We were both so wrung out afterwards that all we did for the next two weeks was cuddle.

"All right, fine," Ravi said. "Hard to top that. It wasn't the best day of your life. It *was* your best party ever."

Especially once Jake had shown up on my doorstep.

"All joking aside, Ben, your boy toy is turning forty. It's a big deal! Am I right?" He aimed this over my shoulder at the guy who was back on his unsubtle mission of trying to steal the stool out from under me.

"Huh?" The guy yelled, taking the opportunity to brace an arm beside my face and nudge me an inch closer to the edge of the seat.

I growled and hooked my ankles around the legs of the stool.

"Forty!" Ravi bellowed back. "Turning forty! It's a big deal!"

"Oh, yeah. Definitely."

"You leave him out of it," I said to Ravi, and sent the guy another glare.

He grinned at me.

"You're not having my stool," I said.

He shrugged again, and turned back to his friend.

"Maybe Jake doesn't want it to be a big deal. I didn't. Also, stop calling him my boy toy. He's three years younger than me. We're practically the same age."

"Ben. Come on."

"We are!"

"I mean, come on about the party."

"I don't know," I hedged.

"*I* know. Yes. Say yes. Trust me, you want to say yes." His eyes glittered. "It's a fantastic idea. Yes."

"Of course you'd say that. Any excuse for a party."

"A fair point," Ravi said, and broke off for a quick swig of his Guinness. He reached out easily and caught my shoulder when the person behind knocked me forwards.

"Do you mind?" I snarled. It was a different guy this time, but he was as unconcerned about personal space as the previous one.

I opened my eyes wide at Ravi, who just shook his head at me like I was the one with the attitude problem.

"It's a fantastic idea, and the only reason you don't want to agree is because you're a party pooper," he said.

"Guilty as charged."

Ravi twisted his pint glass idly on the beermat. Another load of people had spilled into the cramped pub, and he had to raise his voice over a bright burst of laughter from a group of shirts-and-ties behind us to be heard. Someone had rage-quit, apparently, and his friends were all toasting his freedom. "Are you really so selfish that you're going to deny your man his special day?"

"I'm not denying him—"

"Are you soooo selfish that you're going to put your party preferences above Jake's, and let this momentous occasion pass on by, unmarked?"

"I haven't put my preferences above his, I'm still thinking about your stupid idea. And I am *not* selfish," I added indignantly. "I empty the dishwasher every single time, Ravi. Every. Single. Time. Without complaining." To Jake, anyway. I might have mentioned it to my mother once or twice on our weekly chats. "Do you know what he does if the dishwasher is clean and full, and he has dirty dishes? He puts it all in the sink. Doesn't empty the dishwasher and put them in there. He leaves it. If I didn't empty the thing, it would be an expensive crockery cabinet with a plug, and the sink would be unusable."

"You're a hero." Ravi stared at me over the rim of his pint glass. "Or something."

"I am a hero! I am. You know why? Because I'd happily do that for the next sixty years, because it's Jake."

"Aw. Now that is true love. Also, pretty ambitious of you. You're shooting for a hundred and three?"

"I'm not saying I'm perfect. I'd probably bang a few plates around to make my point that it would be nice if he'd do it every once in a while. I might slam a drawer or too. But I'm not selfish."

"You're saying yes to the party, then."

"I'm not saying yes."

"But you're going to. Because you're not selfish and you think it's an amazing idea."

"Honestly, no. I don't think it's an amazing idea. Personally, I loathe and despise surprise parties—"

Ravi smiled fondly at me. "No, you don't. Drama queen."

"Loathe and despise them, and—"

He snapped up a hand. "Stop. Admit it to me right here and now, Benjamin Porter. We need to get this straightened out once and for all, before we take another step. You loved your party. You love parties in general. The only thing you don't like about parties is organising them yourself, because you always convince yourself no one's going to come even when they've all RSVP'd yes. In fact, next time you have anything big to celebrate and I throw you a surprise party, you'll be thrilled. You'll be all, *Thank you, Ravi, you are the most amazing friend in the whole wide world. You're a party wizard, and you make my life better just by existing. Kiss me.*"

"Fine. You're right. Apart from the *kiss me* bit." We'd tried that when we were thirteen. Once was enough. "The party was great, and if I'd known it was coming, I'd have spent a month obsessing about it. Next milestone, go nuts. Surprise me. You have full permission."

My next milestone was seven years down the road, and I hoped—I prayed—that by the time we hit fifty, Ravi would have calmed down a bit.

"Carte blanche?" Ravi said. "I like it." He sat back and rubbed his hands together. "That's you sorted. Now, let's bring it back to Jake's big day. I have some planning to do."

"Don't go overboard," I warned him.

"Overboard? *Me*? I am the soul of taste and discretion."

"Right. Yes. Taste and discretion."

"I am the *discreetest* man you ever met."

Ravi was six foot one. He favoured tight neon t-shirts that showed off his broad chest and shoulders, had a laugh like a foghorn, an insatiable appetite for shenanigans, and was known as the worst gossip in the entire hospital.

"So discreet," I said.

He waved at the bartender and ordered another round. "Now. The first question is, how big am I going to go with this?"

"Not too big," I said, visions of drone light shows, nineties cover act concerts and glitter cannons making my blood run cold.

"Back off, party pooper. This is Jake's big day. I want to make it memorable for him."

"He's pretty easygoing. I'm sure he'd be happy with some cake and bubbly, like I was."

"Cake and bubbly? Bitch, please. That is entry-level shit. That shit is for amateurs." He gestured at me. "My boy Jake is way more sophisticated in the partying department than you."

He really was. Jake was almost as obnoxiously social as Ravi, which was one of the reasons they fell in disgusting platonic love with each other about two weeks into our relationship.

For a moment there, I thought they were going to run away and get platonically married, and I'd find myself in a throuple.

"Can you at least keep it reasonably simple?" I said. "Don't do anything crap like rent out the ice rink."

Ravi's eyes lit up. "The ice rink," he breathed. "I bet I can get a discount because he works there. Ooh. They already have a killer sound system. It's already set up for parties anyway—"

"Yes, and unless you want it to be an alcohol-free surprise party, forget about it," I said. "They're not going to let a bunch of randos on the ice with blades to go along with their impaired motor control and cognitive function."

Ravi slumped.

"How about we just hire The Lion in town?"

His expression told me what he thought of that.

"The Star?" I tried.

"No pubs. Leave it with me. I'll come up with something that my special boy will never see coming."

I eyed him warily. "Nothing too over the top, though, Ravi. Right?"

"Nothing too over the top. I promise. It will be both tasteful and dignified. An intimate little get-together to mark this momentous, once-in-a-lifetime occasion in a dear friend's life. And If I can mess with said dear friend at the same time, and spring it upon him when he is completely unsuspecting? That's just the inch-thick buttercream icing on the great big pink three-tier cake."

"He gets three tiers? I only had one."

Ravi smiled. "Ben, for your next surprise cake, I'll make it four."

"Thank you."

In retrospect, the warning signs were all right there. I had no excuse. I *knew* this man and his diabolical mind, and I should, at the very least, have been suspicious.

I wasn't.

More fool me.

8

*J*ake was being weird.

He'd got back an hour ago from a work trip to Sheffield, having accompanied one of his skaters up there to a qualifying competition at the Olympic-sized rink. He'd dumped his bags at home and come to meet me at The Star for dinner, and it was a good job that I was already sitting at our table when he joined me, because otherwise the kiss he laid on me would have knocked me clean off my feet.

He pulled back and cupped my face, staring down into my wide eyes.

The world fell away—the latest top-forty hit playing over the speakers fuzzed out to white noise, the sound of people talking and laughing faded to a hum, and the cheerful pub around us blurred until the only thing in focus was Jake.

"Uh," I said stupidly as I tried to remember how to breathe. "Hi. Hello. Glad to be home?"

"You have no idea." His hungry gaze roamed over my face, as if he hadn't seen me for a year.

I caught his wrists, frowning when I felt the rapid beat of his pulse under my fingertips. "Are you okay?"

He bent down and kissed me again. This one was short, fierce, and no less overwhelming. He pulled away, changed his mind and darted back in for one more, then collapsed into the chair opposite.

"I thought it was a good trip?" I said. His skater had qualified, and nothing made him happier than that. He didn't seem happy. He seemed...off? No, not off. But not himself, either.

"It was a great trip. I just...I'm ready, Ben. I'm really, really ready." His voice throbbed. "To be home."

"Right." I eyed him. His cheeks were flushed and he was staring at me. His dark eyes were heavy.

Oh.

I knew *that* look.

I shifted on my chair. "Do you...? Do you want to skip dinner and go home right now? We can always order pizza instead, if you—"

"*No.*"

I straightened, somewhat taken aback by his vehemence. "Okaaay. Thai?"

"No, I mean..." He swallowed hard and rubbed his hands over his face. "Sorry. I'm a bit wound up."

"Jake, are you sure you're okay?"

"Yes! I'm fine. I'm better than fine, I'm great." He stretched a hand out across the table, reaching for me. I reached back, and he tangled our fingers together. "I'm excited to be here, that's all." He lifted my hand to his lips and kissed it.

Someone was *really* in the mood tonight.

Jake hid a smile against my hand. The light abrasion of

his stubble over my skin sent a wave of goosebumps rippling down my arm.

My fingers tightened on his. "No to pizza and Thai. How about Chinese? We could—"

"No," he said. "We need to stick to the plan. Dinner here. And then, when I get you home..." He trailed off into a deliberate and meaningful silence, backed up with a serious smoulder.

I raised my brows. "Don't stop there," I said. "When you get me home, what? Can I expect something fun?"

He grinned and slouched lower in his seat. "Mm-hmm."

"Any hints?"

"It's a surprise," he said, looking very pleased with himself.

"I hope you realise that you're setting some pretty high expectations. If all I get after this is the same old Saturday night special, I'll be disappointed." I absolutely would not be disappointed. I loved his Saturday night special. I loved him and what he did to me any night of the week. Or day. I wasn't fussy. "You'd better deliver."

"Oh, I will, Ben. I will."

Bizarrely enough, he sounded both threatening and nervous when he said it, which made a peculiar combination for Jake.

Had he been looking things up on the internet again, I wondered, and would I be able to walk tomorrow?

Not that I cared. Tomorrow was Sunday. I didn't have to go anywhere. I could have a long lie in and insist he brought me breakfast in bed, just like I usually did.

His intensity eased somewhat as we ate, but he continued to give me little touches and hot looks all throughout the meal, with the result that by the time I was tucking into dessert, I was as wound up as he was.

I didn't mess around with my apple crumble, packing it efficiently away under his intense focus. I'd nobly offered to forgo it for once so we could get home all the sooner, but he wasn't a stupid man, and he didn't take me up on it.

Nina, our earnest teenage server, bounced up with the card reader less than a second after I'd set my spoon down beside my empty bowl. While things were relaxed at The Star during the week, on a Saturday night tables were in demand, and she was ready to hustle us out the door and seat the next customers.

I opened my mouth to ask for the bill, and snapped it shut when Jake spoke first. "Two coffees, please, Nina."

I don't know who was more surprised, me or Nina.

"Sure, guys," she said brightly. "Be right with you." She gather up my empty bowl and trotted off to the kitchen.

"I take it I need the extra stimulant to get through whatever awaits me at home?" I said.

Jake's smile was slow and filthy. "It can't hurt."

"You know I won't sleep until after midnight if I drink coffee this late," I warned him. "I don't want to hear any complaints about fidgeting."

"Ben." He leaned forwards and touched my cheek. I managed not to nuzzle into his hand, but it was a close-run thing. "Trust me, you won't be sleeping until at least three a.m., and it won't be the coffee keeping you awake."

My stomach plunged.

"Did you want decaf?" Nina said helpfully from beside my shoulder.

I cleared my throat. "No, thanks," I said. "Just the usual."

We sat and drank our coffee, Nina shooting us impatient looks every time she bustled past. For a moment, I thought that Jake was going to order another round but when I came back from the gents, our table was occupied by another

First Dates and Birthday Cakes | 109

couple and Nina was jotting down their order on her notepad.

I spotted Jake waiting by the exit and headed over.

One of the best things about living in a small town like Chipping Fairford was that everything was in walking distance. We'd bought a house together last year on the outskirts of town and it took longer to get home from the pub than it used to, but I was more than happy to wend my way through the soft twilight streets, holding hands and talking quietly.

Well.

Usually I was happy to do so.

Tonight, there was no wending.

Jake set a pace that was more power walk than evening stroll, and he gripped my hand so tightly as he dragged me along after him that I eventually had to ask him to ease up before he ground my bones to dust.

The heated looks that had been put on the back burner while we ate were once again up to a full boil, and I felt his attention on the side of my face the whole way. I started to blush. His eyes were hot and glittering in the dusk, glinting in the streetlights, and he was unashamedly staring.

In a carnal way.

Or in what I misinterpreted as a carnal way.

It was actually emotional and a little bit panicked, although I didn't realise it right then, what with being all-in and fully onboard with the carnal situation.

We made it home in record time and I couldn't wait any longer. As soon as we hit the doorstep, I turned and stretched up to kiss him.

"Mmm." He smiled against my mouth.

Sliding a hand to the back of his neck, I pulled him

closer. He staggered and bumped into me, squashing me against the door.

I kissed him deeper, rolling my hips into his and...rolling them into the air? Jake pulled away from the kiss with a very unsexy smacking sound, and unwound my arms from around his shoulders.

"What's wrong?" I said, still staring at his mouth.

"Let's take it inside."

"Right. Yes." I glanced around. There was no one out here to see us, but considering the way things tended to escalate once he got his tongue—or anything else—in my mouth, it was the smart move.

I opened the door after a couple of fumbling tries, very aware of his big body thrumming with tension behind me, of his heat sinking into me, and stumbled across the threshold.

I'd left the kitchen light on when we went out, but Jake must have closed the door when he dropped his bags off earlier, as the hall was dark. He pulled the front door shut, and I jumped him. I had my hands on his arse and my mouth on his the second he faced me.

He moaned quietly, returning the kiss with desperation, and then he pulled away again, easing me back.

I dropped flat to the floor and gazed up at him suspiciously. "What's going on with you?" I said.

"Nothing."

"You're being weird tonight."

"No, I'm not."

"I mean, I'm fine with it. I don't care. I like it weird. You *know* I like it weird."

Jake laughed. Loudly and a little hysterically, his eyes flicking to the side.

"Ohhhh," I said. "Is that what this is about?"

"No, I—"

"You want it weird tonight, baby?"

Jake sucked in a breath, eyes going large.

"Yeah?" I said. I shimmied up to him and plastered myself against his front. "How weird are we talking? You want me to open my toy box and get out the—"

He bent his head and kissed me hard, muffling the rest of my words.

I moaned into his mouth, making it nice and theatrical.

Jake liked to hear me make some noise. He got off on my enthusiasm, which was a good thing, as more often than not, he had me wailing.

I bit his bottom lip and dragged it between my teeth—slow, gentle, and filthy.

Releasing him, I said, "And since it's your birthday next week, as a special treat, we can go as hard as you want this time. I won't even mind if you want to try putting *two* of them, right up my—"

He clapped a hand over my mouth.

I blinked up at him, startled.

Narrowing my eyes, I grasped his wrist and drew it slowly away. "Okay," I said. "We can stick with one, that's fine, we—oh my god." The last bit was muffled, because he covered my mouth again.

I tossed my head and *mmphed*, but I couldn't shake him off. He looked like he was trying not to laugh. I went still, and raised a brow.

Very slowly, he slipped his hand away.

I could read between the lines. "If you're trying to tell me you want to gag me, then—"

Oh, this was getting ridiculous.

Jake's hand was back over my mouth, and he'd moved to

stand behind me. One arm was around my waist, and he pulled my head back to rest on his shoulder.

I writhed against him. In a sexy way, not to get free.

He choked and arched his hips away.

Rude. *Now* I wanted to get free.

I bit his hand and he yelped, letting go.

I turned to face him, putting my hands on my hips and glaring.

In the low light, Jake looked like he was torn between laughter and some other emotion I couldn't quite put my finger on.

"I've changed my mind," I informed him crisply. "Hot, nasty, it's-nearly-your-birthday-and-you-can-go-to-town-on-all-of-this-however-you-want sex is off the table. You clearly don't want it weird. That's fine. You know what you get? Vanilla sex. That's it."

"God, I hope you're still saying that later tonight," he said with feeling. "Come here."

"What are you—"

He opened the front door and hustled me out.

"What on earth are you doing?" I demanded as he pulled the door shut and pressed me up against it.

"Improvising."

"Improvising *what*?"

"Uh." He ducked to kiss me and I jerked my head away. He sighed. "Adjusting. I didn't mean improvising, I meant I'm adjusting my plan for the evening. I didn't see it going quite like this."

"Too late. I offered weird and you shot me down. Now I've adjusted *my* plan for the evening, and that plan is, you're getting a big old serving of vanilla."

He shifted his weight. "Ben, can you keep your voice down?" he said. "Just a tiny bit?"

First Dates and Birthday Cakes | 113

I ignored him. "Vanilla. The most boring flavour of all. You know what? This sex is going to be so boring, I might even fall asleep in the middle of it. I'd say feel free to go ahead and keep thrusting, but that's probably too kinky for you, what with being all about the vanilla. You'll just have to pull out and deal with blue balls."

"*Ben,*" he said on a desperate-sounding giggle.

"Oh no, sweetheart. We are going to have sex that is so incredibly dull," I threatened. "I'll lie there and say things like, *yum. That's so nice. Ooh.* We'll gaze tenderly into each other's eyes. You heard me. Soul gazing. That's what's on the cards for you tonight. There *was* going to be bouncing and moaning. Now it's soul gazing. If you're lucky and I don't fall asleep in the middle of it, I might lean up and give you a sweet little kiss on the lips to encourage you. Probably not, though."

"Ben, this really, really isn't the time to be discussing our sex life."

"I think it's the perfect time."

"No." He stepped into me, snatched me against him and clamped his hand over my mouth. Again.

What was his deal, seriously?

"Do you trust me?" he said.

I rolled my eyes at him and nodded.

"Okay. I'm going to take my hand away and you're not going to mention our...intimate relations...at all."

Intimate relations?

"Okay?" he asked. "I have something I really need to get off my chest here, something I've been wanting to say for a while, and talking about bouncing and moaning and making it weird isn't the vibe I'd had in mind for this specific moment. At all. Okay?"

"Okay," I said against his hand.

He cautiously removed it.

We stared at each other in silence. I blinked at the look in his eyes—open, raw, and intense. Even though the diffused light from the street light nearby was dim, I could see it all shining through.

"Ben." He touched my cheek softly. "I love you."

I smiled at him. "And I love—"

"Shh."

"My god. Am I not allowed to talk at all?"

"It would probably be for the best."

"Fine. Sorry. Carry on."

He lowered himself to the doorstep.

Now, normally when Jake went to his knees before me, I could expect a swift unbuttoning and unzipping, and I'd be the delighted recipient of one of his top-notch blowjobs. Since we were outside, I was about to stop him, but then it hit me.

He went down on one knee, not two.

And his hand went into his own trousers, not mine.

My heart skipped a beat.

When he pulled his hand out, he was holding a small square box. He flicked it open with a thumb, and held up to me. "Ben Porter, will you marry me?" A classic, plain gold band sat in the box.

I opened my mouth but no sound came out.

He began to smile.

I took his face in my shaking hands, bent down, and kissed him.

Our lips parted softly and we...okay, fine.

We soul gazed.

"Well?" he said. "Was that a yes?"

"What do you think?"

"It seemed promising. But I'd like to hear you say it."

"Yes," I said.

Jake surged to his feet, caught my chin, and lifted my mouth to his. He kissed me and kissed me, until I was laughing and clutching his shoulders to stay upright.

"Come on," I said when his kisses got more desperate, more demanding. "Come on, let's go inside." I wasn't sure why he'd decided to propose on the doorstep, and right now, I didn't care. All I cared about was getting some privacy. I fumbled behind me for the door handle.

"In a minute," he said, stopping me.

"Okay," I said breathlessly. "Oh. Yes. The ring!"

He'd taken it out of the box, stuffed the box in his pocket, and lifted my hand. "May I?"

"Please do." I shivered when he slid it slowly down my finger.

It felt strange. Cold and heavy.

I was never taking it off.

Jake stared down at my hand, which he had gripped between his and was holding between us. "I'm starting to regret this."

"That's got to be the fastest case of buyer's remorse in all of human history," I said.

I'd have panicked, except the look on his face didn't match his words. The look on his face wasn't even close to regret. On the contrary, it was a look I was very familiar with. It was tight with need and hard with possession. It screamed: *mine*.

That was not the look of a man who had changed his mind, despite how it sounded.

"No," he said quickly, and lifted my hand. He kissed the back of it fiercely. "Not this. Never this. Never you."

"I know," I said, smiling up at him.

"Do you?"

"Yes." I shrugged. I wasn't certain about many things in life, but Jake's love was impossible to doubt. "So, if not this —*oh*—" he kissed my hand again, lips curving against it and eyes flaring when he saw what it did to me, "—then what exactly are you regretting? Proposing on the doorstep? Or... was that like a thing? A symbolic thing?"

He looked thoughtful. "That makes sense, doesn't it?"

"Yes. We're on the threshold of the next phase of our lives. I think it's romantic. Good job."

"It *is* romantic," he said. "Or it could make a nice callback to our first kiss."

"Our first kiss was at the ice rink. You just lost a point on that one."

"First kiss with tongue."

"Less romantic, but okay." I looked at him suspiciously. "That's not the reason, is it?"

"No. Nope. Sorry. Going forward, though, whenever we tell people this story, let's say that's why."

"All right. Are you going to let me in on the real reason?"

The heat in his eyes shifted towards amusement. "I want you to remember that you love me."

"I will never forget," I vowed.

"And remember that this right here, this moment between us, was a romantic and beautiful moment."

"Etched into my memory," I assured him.

"God, I love you." He dropped a quick kiss on my lips, straightened, and said, "Okay. Here it is. I may have got carried away when we were planning this whole thing."

"I like it when you get carried away, and—wait."

His words sank in.

...when we were planning....

...when we...

...we...

A yawning chasm of horror opened up deep inside me. "*We*? We who?"

"I didn't mean to tell him, Ben," Jake said. "I had a moment of weakness, and next thing I knew, everything had spun out of control. You know what he's like."

"*No*," I said.

"He floated the idea of celebrating your next big milestone and everything with you on Thursday, and said that you were fully on board with it. *Carte blanche* were his exact words. Or I never would have agreed."

I gazed up into Jake's face. He knew I'd forgive him anything, but he had the grace to look a little nervous, at least. "You bastard."

He grinned. Probably because my lips were twitching. "It sounded like such a good idea in theory. I was going to propose, give Ravi the signal, and then…" He trailed off.

"Finish, please," I said, holding onto his sides and digging my fingers in.

"Then the friends and family gathered in the kitchen would leap out, and *ta-da!* Surprise engagement party. You'd get all the fun of it but none of the buildup, which you hate. It was going to be seamless. And magical. Or something."

"It's definitely something."

"But as soon as we got into the hall, I realised…" He broke off and gazed down at me. "I realised that I may have made a mistake."

"Just to clarify, not the whole bit about proposing?"

"God, no," he said. "You are mine for good. No take backs."

"Yeah," I whispered, stretching up to kiss him.

I should probably pace myself here. I was, after all, going to get to kiss him for the rest of my life. No need to wear my lips out on day one of happily ever after.

Just one more, though.

I always wanted one more.

He stroked my cheek and ran the back of his fingers along my jaw and down the side of my neck. "I thought about everyone in the kitchen listening, and I didn't want them to hear it."

"Good call," I said. "I wouldn't have wanted them to hear —" I broke off. "Oh my god." The hands I had been gently smoothing up and down his sides turned into claws of desperation and I dug in. "*Jake.*"

"What is it?" His eyes widened.

"*They heard me talking about our sex life.*"

"No, no," he said. "I'm sure they didn't."

"Why didn't you stop me!"

"I did try."

"Not hard enough. Not nearly hard enough!"

"Calm down. No one heard anything. The kitchen door was shut. I made Ravi promise. It was part of the plan. Party to celebrate, yes. Audience for the actual proposal, no."

"If you're so sure they can't hear then why did you bring us out here, huh?"

He winced. "Nobody heard. And if they did, then it wasn't that bad."

"It was bad!"

He started laughing.

I shoved him. "I can't believe you."

He swayed back towards me and leaned his full weight against me. "How was I to know you'd get all sexy and try to seduce me the minute we walked in the door?"

"It's Saturday night and I'm wearing my get-me-some jeans, that's how. Also, don't pretend like you haven't been eye-fucking me for the last two and a half hours. You *know* what that kind of eye contact does to me!"

First Dates and Birthday Cakes | 119

"Ben." He tipped my chin up and gazed down at me. "Nobody heard. You weren't that loud—"

"I was loud! You told me to keep my voice down! That means I was loud!"

"You weren't that loud."

I was loud. I'd done it on sexy purpose!

"They were all in the kitchen, behind a shut door. And even if they *did* hear, then the worst they'd have heard was you offering to give it to me weird." He only just managed to get that last bit out before he dissolved into very unmanly giggles.

"That is still off the table," I said, desperately trying to believe him.

And really, it wasn't that bad. Everyone knew we had a sex life. There is no shame in it. Did my mother need to hear things like that? No. Had she heard—and seen— worse? Sadly, yes. She once walked in on me as a teenager when I was fooling around with Harvey Wheeler, the son of Dad's veterinary nurse.

More than once, she walked in on me fooling around with myself, until my dad took pity on me and quietly installed a lock on my bedroom door.

But that had been when I was a teenager!

"Are you sure?" Jake said. "Because I think I can convince you to change your mind."

"I doubt it."

"No? You mean after we've gone in there and put them out of their misery, you won't let me have it? Vanilla, weird, however I want it?"

"Why are they miserable?"

"They're going to think you said no, we've been out here so long."

"A*ha*," I said. "I mean, I could have said no." I poked him in the chest. "This is why proposing in front of other people is a terrible idea. You're either pressuring the other person to say yes so they don't cause a scene, or you're risking embarrassment in front of everyone you know."

He caught my poking finger. "I didn't propose in front of other people. Ravi suggested it—"

"He is *such* a drama ho, seriously."

"—but I said absolutely not. This bit is between you and me."

"Mm-hmm. And the ten people earwigging in my kitchen. All of whom," I added indignantly, "got the memo about us getting hitched before I did."

"Ten people," he said, and winced again.

"More than ten?"

"Listen, I've already told you that I got carried away, and I am sorry. I don't know what came over me. I suppose I got swept up in the idea of, you know." He had his hands on my hips and he firmed his grip, pulling me closer. "Winning you."

"Winning me?"

"Yeah."

"Like a prize?"

"Yeah. I'm good enough to snag Ben Porter. I want the world to know."

The astonishing thing was, he wasn't even being funny about it. He didn't say it wryly, or with a twinkle in his eye or with a curl to his lips that said he was fighting back a smile.

He meant it.

My heart turned over. "Like you just competed in the Olympics and I'm the gold medal?"

He bit his lip and nodded.

I curled my hand around the back of his neck and drew

him down to me, pressing our mouths together. "That's incredibly flattering," I murmured.

"It's the truth."

"Well," I said, "I regret to inform you that you didn't actually win gold on this occasion. You're in second place with silver. Because I'm the one on the podium with the gold medal."

"What?" he said, pulling back and scowling at me.

I really misjudged that one. *And* his competitiveness. I widened my eyes at him. "You," I said. "You're the gold medal."

"No, Ben, I *won* the gold medal. Which is you."

I hid my smile. "I beg to differ."

"No, I...Ben. This is my metaphor. Don't ruin it. I won the Olympic gold medal in boyfriends."

"It's my metaphor. You just said I was a prize. I was the one who brought up the Olympics."

His scowl deepened.

"I'm waving to the crowd," I said, and threw up a triumphant arm, waving to an imaginary audience behind him. "Everyone's clapping and cheering."

He growled and hauled my arm down. "Stop it. *I* won the gold medal."

"Don't be a sore loser. Silver is nothing to sneer at."

He pinned my arms to my sides and bit my neck.

My knees went weak and I sagged against the door. "That's cheating," I said.

"Don't care. I'll cheat, I'll be a sore loser, I'll take silver instead of gold...I don't even care. So long as I've got you. That's the only thing that matters."

"You have me," I said, holding him tight. "You have me."

He squeezed me hard against his body, then let out a

huge sigh. "I really do regret this," he said. "I'm not in the mood for a party right now—"

"You mean a victory parade?" I said sweetly.

"All I want is to drag you upstairs and spend the next few hours making you scream. Ah, well. Live and learn. I'm not going to let Ravi anywhere near our wedding, I'll tell you that much." He opened the door and walked me backwards through it.

I did my best to smooth my hair down, and checked that all my buttons were buttoned and zips zippered. My lips felt hot and puffy and I was pretty sure I had stars in my eyes to match the ones in Jake's, but there wasn't anything I could do about that now.

"You ready?" Jake said.

"Yes. Let's do it. What's the signal?"

Jake drew me into the sitting room after him , took a deep breath, and said loudly, "He said yes!"

"That's inventive," I muttered, and he elbowed me.

I braced in anticipation of the door bursting open and Ravi hosing us down with champagne.

Nothing happened.

We exchanged glances.

Jake raised his voice. "He said yes!"

Still nothing.

"Wait there." He strode across to the kitchen door and snatched it open, saying, "You missed the sig...huh."

"Huh?" I followed him, and stared into the kitchen. "Huh."

It was empty.

Well. Empty of people.

The kitchen island was an absolute riot of flowers and cake and balloons, a huge silver ice bucket with champagne chilling, and a tray with two glasses on it, tied together with a big pink ribbon.

"What?" Jake said, bewildered.

I shoved him out of my way and beelined for the cake.

"Oh my god," I said. "Look at this thing."

It was, I shit you not, two feet tall. It was twice as big as the one he'd bought for my fortieth birthday. It looked like a wedding cake.

Scratch that, it *was* a wedding cake.

It was a gorgeous, delicious-looking monster of a wedding cake. A great big four-tier pink concoction with buttercream icing and sequins.

There were even two little men in tuxedos on the top. They were wearing ice skates. It was easy to tell which one was supposed to be Jake and which one was supposed to be me, because one of them was bent over laughing, and the other one was facedown in the buttercream.

My skating hadn't improved much since we first met, despite Jake's best efforts. I was great at falling, though.

I'd never seen a cake that big in real life.

It was bigger than my cousin Sophie's cocker spaniel.

"Where is everyone?" Jake said, confused.

"Not here." I darted to the cutlery drawer and snatched a knife out of the block above it. "Who cares?" I eyed the cake, reconsidered, and got a bigger knife.

"He was supposed to...I mean, he said he'd bring a cake, but this is...this is a lot."

"I know," I said gleefully. "We'll be eating it for a month. Do you want to cut it or shall I?"

Jake hooked a finger in the ice bucket and tipped it towards him. He grunted. "Ice hasn't melted."

"Okay, Sherlock. What does that mean?"

"It means someone was here not that long ago."

We stared at each other.

"Do you think they all ran away because we took so long and they thought I said no?" I said.

My dad would have headed the charge out the backdoor. He had a problem with secondhand embarrassment, which truly was a cross to bear, considering me and my mother.

"No," Jake said. He picked up the obnoxiously large card propped beside the ice bucket and scanned it. "This was a double bluff."

He passed me the card.

It was from Ravi.

Happy Engagement, my friends.

PS: Ben, I told you I was the discreetest person you ever met.

PPS: Jake, I told you I knew how to throw the perfect engagement party.

PPPS: Enjoy, losers!

"That dick," Jake said with feeling.

I laughed. "Did you want to have loads of people here?"

"No. Like I said, I regretted the whole idea practically at once but I felt, you know. Committed. And then Ravi just kept texting me about it. He wouldn't let up. I should have suspected something."

"Of course you should. It's Ravi. Then again, I've known him since I was three years old and I still fall for his shit. Don't beat yourself up."

"It was pretty obvious, now I think about it. He said he'd take care of everything, and all I had to do was on pain of death not to even mention it to anyone because he wanted everyone to think it would be a huge surprise to both of us. Which—" he waved an arm around the kitchen, "—it obviously was."

I smiled. "No one else knows," I said confidently.

"What?"

"That's why he did it." I looped my arms around his waist and eased him around so his arse was propped against the edge of the island. "He knew that I'd be pissed off if I was the last to know about my own engagement."

Jake grimaced. "The more I think about it, the more I realise what a terrible idea this was in the first place. I bought the rings six months ago, Ben. It's taken me that long to get up the nerve to ask you."

I gazed up at him. *Get up the nerve?* "Did you really think I'd say no?"

"No. Still, some part of me wakes up next to you every day and my first thought is, *I can't believe I get to wake up next to this man.*"

I shook my head.

"Yeah," he said, tilting up my chin and holding it. "I love you. Six months I hid that box in my gym bag."

Wise choice. The one place I'd never go.

"Sometimes, I was walking around with it in my pocket. I nearly proposed once when we were watching *Jurassic World* for the hundredth time, but you told me to shush because it was getting to the good bit."

It was my favourite movie, and I wouldn't apologise for it. I never claimed to have good taste.

Except in men.

My taste in men was stellar.

I couldn't really wrap my head around the idea that he'd been trying to 'get up the nerve' to ask me to marry him, and he'd been on the brink of it for six months while I'd been blithely going about my day, doing things like putting the bins out, hanging up laundry, lounging on the sofa with my head on his lap while watching velociraptors cheerfully murder people.

I *really* couldn't wrap my head around the fact that Ravi

had somehow managed to surprise us both with an engagement party that was supposed to be a surprise only to me.

He truly was a party wizard.

I'd never hear the end of it.

"So," I said.

"So?"

"Shall we get this party started?"

Jake flexed against me. "What did you have in mind?"

"Are you kidding?" I gestured at the cake. "*Obviously* we'll start with—" Jake ducked his head and kissed me. "Or," I said breathlessly when he pulled back, "we save the cake and the bubbly until after."

"I like the sound of that."

~END~

ALSO BY ISABEL MURRAY

Romantic Comedy

Not That Complicated

Not That Impossible

Worth the Wait

Merman Romance

Catch and Release

Fantasy Romance

Gary of a Hundred Days

Gary the Once and Former King

The Naiad's Gift

NOT THAT COMPLICATED EXCERPT

Chapter One

It wasn't exactly crowded in the pub, even though it was lunchtime. It was a cold Tuesday in February, in the Cotswolds. We didn't get many tourists at this time of year, and at least half the population of Chipping Fairford had dragged themselves off to the train station at six a.m. for the grim commute into London, while those of us smart enough to work from home were gleefully still in bed.

In other words, there was more than enough room at the bar. So why the guy who'd just blown in on a cold blast of rain-scented air felt it necessary to shove himself right up beside me, I had no idea. He was so close, I could feel his body heat, and smell his rather nice shampoo.

I eased to the side, putting some distance between us, and did my best to catch Lenny the bartender's eye. When Lenny had finished pulling a pint of Guinness for the glum-looking man I thought was my postie, he glanced my way.

And his eyes skimmed right over me to land on the newcomer instead.

I scowled.

For god's sake. It wasn't like we were in a crowded nightclub where the hot guys get served first.

Then I turned to the guy beside me and thought, okay. Wow. *He* belongs in a nightclub.

The invitation-only kind, populated by actors, models, minor royals, and Beyonce.

The loose curls of his thick, red-gold hair lay in a sexy, tousled mop that sparkled with scattered raindrops. A fashionably beat-up leather jacket hung open to show a navy t-shirt that clung lovingly to his broad chest and lean torso, and his full lips were curved in a smile as I...

...as I gawked up at him like an idiot.

The smile slowly grew.

Mesmerised, I continued to gawk.

Who knows how long I'd have stayed there, frozen, if Lenny hadn't broken the spell. "Usual for you, Adam?"

At the sound of his name, I recoiled.

You'd think Adam had suddenly lunged at me with bared fangs. I hadn't meant to be dramatic; it was pure protective instinct as my brain finally caught up, put the name together with the face, and I realised exactly who I was gawking at.

It had taken long enough. Then again, the last time I saw Adam was a year ago and he'd looked very different, what with being wet and naked in my shower.

His bright hair, saturated with water, had been a sleek dark bronze. He'd been even more intimidatingly beautiful without clothes on.

And he hadn't been smiling.

Kind of like now.

The smile had dropped clean off his face. "Ray was next," he said to Lenny in a deep voice.

The voice I'd have recognised in an instant. The last time I'd heard it, he was saying, *Yeah. Like that. Just like that. Deeper. Now suck it. Good.*

He hadn't been saying it to me.

He'd been saying it to my boyfriend.

I was the horrified idiot in the bathroom doorway, home unexpectedly early and struggling to process the fact that my boyfriend was on his knees for the checkout boy from the Co-op.

If you wanted to get technical about it, the last time I heard Adam speak was actually when he showed up on my doorstep the next day with an *I'm so, so sorry,* and an *I didn't know, he said he was single,* and a *Can I please—*

I'd slammed the door in his face.

"Ray?" Lenny said. "*Ray.*"

"Huh?"

Lenny looked from me to Adam and back again with sky-high eyebrows. "What can I get you?" he asked.

"A glass of Chenin Blanc and an IPA, please."

I proceeded to stare at Lenny helplessly as he leaned into his forearms on the bar and reeled off a list of ten different IPAs, with names that ran the gamut from sounding like vaguely threatening sex positions to fantasy novel titles generated by an enthusiastic but confused AI.

I was at the pub for a business lunch with my favourite client, Paulina, who'd stopped in for a rare face-to-face meeting en route to a conference in Milton Keynes. The IPA was for her. I had *no* clue.

"The Hobgoblin is good," Adam said about twenty seconds into my blank silence.

I did my best not to shiver, but the hairs on my arms lifted anyway. "In that case, I'll take the Threshing Orc, thanks," I said, grabbing one at random.

It sounded like an advanced sex position *and* a fantasy novel. A decent choice for Paulina, who was very much into both of those things.

"Oh-*kay*," Lenny said, looking from me to Adam and back again before he shook his head and ambled off.

I did my very best not to fidget as I waited.

Adam was staring at me. I *knew* he was. I literally felt his attention go up and down my face like a warm stroke. Huffing out a breath of irritation, I tipped my head to glare up at him.

And he—oh. He wasn't glaring back. His expression was wary. Almost...soft?

"Hi, Ray," he said.

"Go fuck yourself, Adam," I said. Oh, shit. Where did that come from?

Adam's hazel eyes flared. "Mm. Already did that twice this morning. Once in bed when I woke up, and once in the shower. Maybe I can fit something in after lunch, though." He ran his gaze over my trembling body. "I'm certainly in the mood for it now."

ABOUT THE AUTHOR

Isabel Murray is a writer, a reader, and a lover of love. She couldn't stick to a subgenre if her life depended on it, but MM romance is her jam. She lives in the UK, reads way too much, and cannot be trusted anywhere near chocolate.

You can find Isabel at her website, or on Goodreads, Amazon, and Bookbub.

www.isabelmurrayauthor.wordpress.com